Understanding Art

A Reference Guide to Painting, Sculpture, and Architecture
in the Romanesque, Gothic, Renaissance, and Baroque Periods

Volume 1

Understanding Art

A Reference Guide to Painting, Sculpture, and Architecture
in the Romanesque, Gothic, Renaissance, and Baroque Periods

Volume 1

SHARPE REFERENCE
ARMONK, NEW YORK

FITZROY DEARBORN PUBLISHERS
LONDON

SHARPE REFERENCE

Sharpe Reference is an imprint of M.E. Sharpe, Inc.
M.E. Sharpe, Inc.
80 Business Park Drive
Armonk, NY 10504

FITZROY DEARBORN PUBLISHERS
11 Rathbone Place
London W1P 1DE
England

Library of Congress Cataloging-in-Publication Data

Arte come riconoscere. English
Understanding art: a reference guide to painting, sculpture, and architecture in the Romanesque, Gothic, Renaissance, and Baroque periods.
p. cm.
Includes bibliographical references and index.
ISBN 0-7656-8024-6 (alk. paper)
1. Art, Medieval. 2. Art, Renaissance. 3. Art, Baroque.
N5940.A7813 1999
709'.2--dc21
99-15944
CIP

Cataloging-in-Publication Data is also available from the British Library

Printed and bound in Italy

The paper used in this publication meets the minimum requirements of American National Standard for Information Sciences – Permanence of Paper for Printed Library Materials, ANSI Z 39.48-1984

Italian text preparation supervised by:
Flavio Conti (Romanesque, Renaissance, Baroque)
Maria Cristina Gozzoli (Gothic)
Drawings: Mariarosa Conti, Fulvio Cocchi, Franco Testa
Translation: Erica and Arthur Propper (Gothic Art), Barbara Fisher (Romanesque)
Sharpe Reference art editor: Esther Clark
Fitzroy Dearborn art editor: Delia Gaze
Cover design by Lee Goldstein

Contents

Introduction

Understanding Art offers readers an easy-to-use reference guide to some of the great art of the western world. These beautifully illustrated volumes provide examples of architecture, sculpture, and painting for four eras in the history of art: Romanesque, Gothic, Renaissance, and Baroque.

Created with the intention of making these styles and their elements accessible to students, these volumes provide a basic art vocabulary with which to understand and appreciate the architecture, sculpture, and painting of these eras. While architecture dominated the earlier periods, with painting and sculpture providing decoration for the great Romanesque churches and Gothic cathedrals, sculpture and painting as individual art forms became more important in the Renaissance and Baroque eras. To facilitate an understanding of the connection between technology, design, and style, each work of art is analyzed to identify the distinctive characteristics and details that place it within a given period. These elements are illustrated with diagrams intended to make clear the purpose and meaning of the terminology used. In this way, the reader can readily develop a vocabulary, both visual and linguistic, that will serve to assist in the appreciation of architecture, sculpture, and painting of each period. Along with the written description, each drawing helps the eye perceive such concepts as the alternating structure of the aisles in a Romanesque church, the verticality of the columnar statues in Gothic cathedrals, the triangular composition of an altarpiece by Raphael, or the curved line of a Baroque façade.

With this wealth of illustrations, clear drawings, and instructive captions, the reader is able to build up a store of images and knowledge that constitute the basis for a greater and wider understanding of Romanesque, Gothic, Renaissance, and Baroque works of art dating from the eleventh to the seventeenth centuries that can be seen and admired in the cities and museums of Europe.

Understanding Art

A Reference Guide to Painting, Sculpture, and Architecture
in the Romanesque, Gothic, Renaissance, and Baroque Periods

Volume 1

Romanesque Art

The use of the term *Romanesque* for the art created during the early Middle Ages in Western Europe was first proposed in 1824 by the French archaeologist De Caumont and was an immediate success. The word was supposed to express two concepts simultaneously. One was the similarity between the formation process of the Romance languages (Spanish, French, Italian), constructed by mixing popular Latin with the idioms of the Germanic invaders, and that of the figurative arts, accomplished in the same countries and at about the same time by combining what remained of the great Roman artistic tradition with barbarian trends and techniques. The second concept was the connection of this new art to that of ancient Rome. This line of reasoning was not entirely accurate. Romanesque art uses both Roman and Germanic elements but also includes Byzantine, Islamic and Armenian elements. Above all, what it created is essentially original. At first the term

Architecture was the most typical artistic expression of the Romanesque period. Though common structural and decorative solutions developed, strong local schools grew up from these. This is one of the most interesting and characteristic Italian Romanesque churches, Sant'Ambrogio in Milan.

Right
Detail of the tympanum of the church of Ste-Madeleine; Vézelay, France. The names of Romanesque sculptors are rarely known, but on examination their works reveal strong personalities.

Romanesque included all the artistic manifestations of Western Europe between the 8th and 13th centuries. But it seemed increasingly arbitrary to use one label for such a broad period of time. The artwork did indeed have many elements in common but also had some fundamental differences. To use the words of the famous art historian Nikolaus Pevsner: "Characteristics, alone, do not make a style. There must be a central idea that gives life to them all." This idea was fully determined in the first two centuries of the new millennium, and it is to this period between the 11th and 13th centuries that we now apply the label *Romanesque*. There were continuations of the style after this, especially on the margins of the places where Romanesque flourished, which at the height of its splendor involved all of western and much of central Europe. Prior to the Romanesque period, there were other artistic periods merit consideration by themselves: Visigothic, Carolingian and Ottonian art (in 8th-century Spain, 9th-century central Europe and 10th-century Germany, respectively).

One last characteristic must be stressed. Although the Romanesque style was quite uniform in many aspects, it was also marked by a large number of local schools that showed regional variations in

applying its basic principles. This fact is in keeping with the social and political conditions of the period but makes its study more complicated. Moreover, stylistic variations are numerous. With the exception of Baroque art, no European figurative experience is more widely present in every country than the Romanesque. Nor is any richer, more vibrant, or more significant.

ARCHITECTURE

The accomplishments of Romanesque architecture are numerous and are found nearly all over Europe. Moreover, they present a very wide range of unusual and regional variations. The elements that are used to identify Romanesque buildings are drawn from this extensive and varied universe. As a result, some guidelines must first be established. Four of these can be indicated fairly precisely and nearly always apply. First, the typical building type is the church, as fundamental to Romanesque architecture as the temple is to the Greek. Second, the entire architectural conception hinges on the solution to a central technical problem: that of covering the enclosed space by means of vaults, that is, curved arches in stone. This encouraged an aesthetic that favored massive articulated structures with strong effects of light and dark, low light penetrating narrow apertures, and coarse

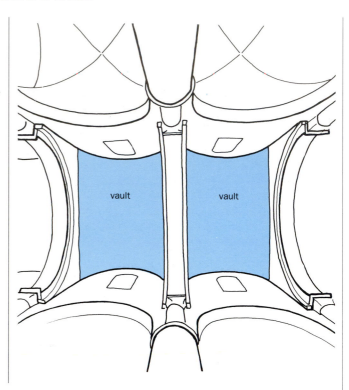

The nave of St-Philibert; Tournus, France.

The predominant theme: the vault

Despite the huge variety of expressions, Romanesque architecture clearly possesses a predominant theme – the covering of the space with stone vaults. This solution was dictated by the need for safety (the prevention of fires, common with wooden roofs) and aesthetic harmony combined with a taste for articulated interiors and exteriors and contrasts made between the various parts of the church.

Opposite page Detail of the vault in the church of Ste-Madeleine, Vézelay.

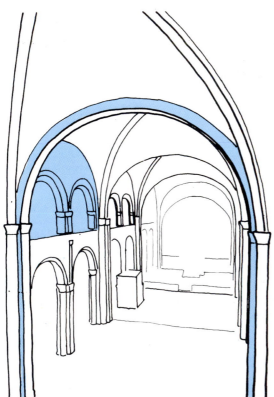

The Lombard system

Romanesque architects elaborated various solutions to resolve the engineering problems posed by the stone-vaulted ceiling. This produces a strong side thrust and must therefore be conceived within a constructional system that absorbs these thrusts. One solution is that seen in the church of Sant'Ambrogio in Milan. The thrust of the vaults of the central nave is countered by side aisles, also covered with vaults and topped with a vaulted tribune; the sum of the thrusts of these small vaults counters that of the main vault.

Interior of the church of Sant'Ambrogio, Milan.

Plan of the church of Sant'Ambrogio, Milan.

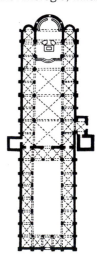

finishing materials. Last, there was a hierarchy in the arts that made architecture the dominant activity, with which all the others – painting, sculpture, mosaics – were subordinate. The first of these characteristics, namely the church as the principal building of the period is not surprising. It could not be otherwise at a time of great, even ardent devotion, when the Catholic Church was by far the richest, most cultured, modernly equipped and widespread organization present. The third and fourth points are valid criteria for identifying buildings of the time. The central and fundamental element is, however, that of the vault. Starting from the characteristics and requirements of a stone vault, the master builders and medieval workers elaborated a system of construction that was consistent in all its parts and formed a style. If the principle is reduced to a minimum, the vault is merely a collection of arches: a curved surface that receives a weight at its highest part and transmits it to the lowest part along a curve that it itself describes. Because of its nature, it may consist of small stones that are mutually

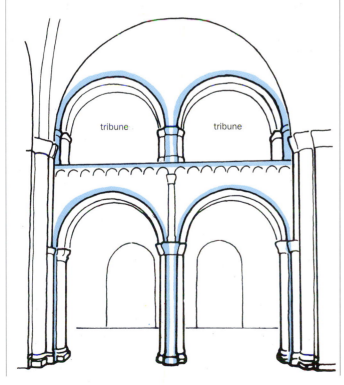

The Lombard system
The system described on the previous page calls for the creation of small minor vaults, at the sides of the high vault, over the aisles and the tribunes. These vaults, with their terminal arches, overlook the great arch created by the profile and piers of the main vault. The appearance of this hierarchy of arched apertures is one of the most characteristic elements of Romanesque architecture and lends rhythm to most of its accomplishments.

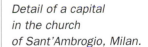

Interior of the church of Sant'Ambrogio, Milan.

Detail of a capital in the church of Sant'Ambrogio, Milan.

balanced, each receiving thrust from the one above it and transmitting it to that below. These thrusts of the vault are discharged onto supports but a side thrust tends to push them outwards. This means that a vault cannot be conceived in isolation. It has to be designed as part of an organism that is capable of absorbing the thrusts it creates. What determines the system is the mutual – and inflexible – play of thrusts and counter-thrusts generated by the shape of the vault.

The Romanesque period adopted various types of vault.

Fairly common, especially in France, was the barrel vault, semicylindrical and the simplest type. But the most typical Romanesque vault is the groin or cross vault. Already known to the Romans, it is produced by crossing two barrel vaults at right angles. The resulting square figure has four semicircular

The alternation of supports
The alternation of supports of different shapes and sizes (compound or cross-shaped piers and cylindrical pillars or columns) in vaulted churches is a consequence of their diverse functions (the piers that sustain only the vault of the side aisles receive a far smaller thrust than those supporting the vault of the main nave, so they are smaller). It often also appears in constructions planned with wooden roofs, where it is far less justified. This is in line with the aesthetic trends of the period.

Top
Façade of the church of San Ciriaco, Ancona.

Opposite page
Nave of the church of San Zeno, Verona.
This is a classic example of Italian Romanesque architecture. There is more attention on the decorative aspect than on constructional consistency. The present wooden roof is Gothic but the church was, perhaps never intended to have a stone vault. Certain elements more typical of vaulted churches, such as the alternation of large piers and minor supports – here columns – that support only the vaults of the side aisles.

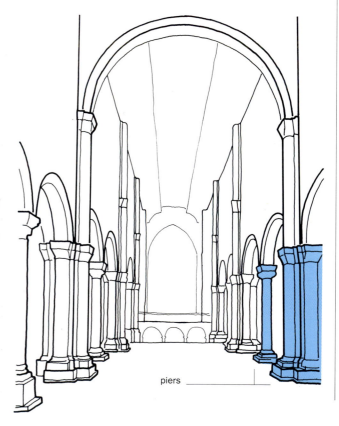

piers

arches at the sides and two elliptical arches along the diagonals. Unlike the barrel vault, which needs to rest on another arch or on a continuous wall, groin vaults require only four points of support, pilasters or columns. If each pilaster is slightly enlarged, it can serve as a point of support for four groin vaults. This is its great advantage – the groin vault can be multiplied in all directions.

Norman Romanesque
Far more refined than the previous system is that elaborated by Norman architects, who above the customary aisles and tribune introduced a third story, the clerestory, to provide lateral illumination in the church.

transverse arch

Opposite page
Durham cathedral in England (conquered in 1066 by the Normans) is the most famous Norman church. It was also probably the first to feature an extremely important aspect of Romanesque architecture: the rib vault. The rib collects most of the structural strain and, continuing down the walls to the ground, creates the characteristic compound pier.

The union of the groin vault with its supports produces the other great feature of Romanesque architecture: the bay. Together these elements form the church. The form and function of the typical Romanesque bay can be described as follows. Four piers are set at the corners of a square and connected by round-headed arches. This unit is then covered by a vault. The round-headed arches defining the bays soon became more pronounced so that responds were attached to the

Top
Detail of a capital in the church of St-Nectaire, France.

Right
Interior of Angoulême cathedral, France.

Left
Interior of Modena cathedral.

Bottom
Capital with the Rivers of Paradise; Musée de Cluny, Paris.

supports to receive them, forming a cross-shaped pier, that is a central nucleus and four projections. This cross-shaped pier is very common in Romanesque buildings but the process can be extended. The two diagonal arches of the vault can also be given a projection that can be continued down to the ground along the pier. This creates four ribs separating the webs of the vault. And, on the ground, each pier will acquire, as well as the central nucleus, eight responds. This is the so-called compound or clustered pier. This

Interior of the cathedral of Santiago de Compostela. There were close cultural, economic and political links between the Christian realms of northern Spain and the towns of southern France, ties intensified by the constant pilgrimages to Santiago de Compostela. The sanctuary was rebuilt from around 1075 onwards, to a plan characteristic of the great French pilgrimage churches, with long, tall naves with tribunes, a broad transept with three aisles and an ambulatory with five apsidal chapels.

THE ROMANESQUE WORKSHOP

The details of Romanesque workshops are still very few and fragmentary, but the *Relatio Translationis Corporis Sancti Geminiani*, with the illustrations that accompany the text, provides a precious account of the hierarchy on the workshop of Modena cathedral. The architect Lanfranco is depicted (see below) sumptuously dressed and armed with a cane (probably both a measuring instrument and a sign of command); he is surrounded by assistants, directing the laying of the building's foundations and giving orders to workers divided into two basic categories: *operarii* and *artifices*. The former appear occupied in the simplest tasks while the latter, possessing more specific technical skills, are finishing the cut stone, laying these stones and bricks or busy at special tasks such as those of the blacksmith or carpenter. The masons' workshop of every great Romanesque construction must have been accompanied by that of the sculptors. At least initially, the sculptors may well have been no more than a special group of *artifices*, but as monumental sculpture became more established, it is very probable that the sculptors who worked stone and marble for interior decorations such as altars, pulpits and screens became increasingly independent. At first a separate group from the stonecutters, entrusted with the decoration of architectural elements (capitals, door frames and so on), they later took on more work, performing it with increasing prestige and autonomy, until they formed a second workshop, with an organization parallel to the architectural one. The sculptors' workshop probably resembled that of the masons, with a master directing operations, flanked by some close assistants, *artifices* and *operarii*.

form of bay, consisting in a cross vault with ribs resting on compound piers is the most typical and refined expression of Romanesque architecture. It has two meanings – one structural and the other aesthetic. Structurally speaking, the invention of the rib was of fundamental importance. It was very quickly realized that the greatest strain of the structure passed through the rib and that practically speaking the webs served more to cover space than truly to support the weight of the vault. This would eventually lead to a distinction between the areas between one

The alternation of supports

In the characteristic differentiation of the supports of the main arcade, the Romanesque style also elaborated various solutions. This example at Worms is, in a certain sense, the reverse of that at Verona. There, a light support – a column – was interposed between heavier supports, the compound piers. Here, the supports are, in conception, all the same – sturdy square piers. However, those supporting the high vaults are more complex, continuing the vault ribs, down to the ground. In both cases the Romanesque characteristic of articulating the space of the church and avoiding a uniform treatment of the supports is clear.

The nave arcade in Worms cathedral.
The churches of the Rhine (Speyer, Mainz, Worms) all have a similar internal design, particularly in the treatment of the main elevation; indeed this method of construction can be considered a distinctive feature of the Romanesque of western Germany. Large square piers divide the main nave from the side aisles and are given elegant semicircular shafts that continue the ribs of the vaults. The details in every church are of course different, as are the dates of construction.

Opposite page
Interior of the church of St. Michael, Hildesheim.

rib and the other (the webs) as nothing more than filling space, something that had to be supported by the ribs. This marked the beginning of the idea that architecture was a load-bearing skeleton covered with a thin layer of marble or glass, later so typical of Gothic architecture (which both continued and went beyond the Romanesque style). In aesthetic, or compositional, terms the bay thus made can be considered the module of Romanesque buildings, that is the element that, repeated

The arch

The typical Romanesque arch is the round-headed, semicircular one, often also used as a decorative motif. A frequent feature in churches is the use of an arch to separate one bay from another, that is, continuing the supports and dividing the vaults that rest on them. This decorative element is sometimes accentuated – as here – by the use of different materials from that employed for the rest of the structure, or the same material in two different colors.

The church of St-Philibert in Tournus is very old and remarkable. The bays (the spaces between piers) are covered with a number of transverse barrel vaults, each arranged parallel to the other. This enables there to be a large window in the head of every vault; the immense lateral thrust that a continuous barrel vault would have produced is avoided, and the sequence of the bays is clearly marked.

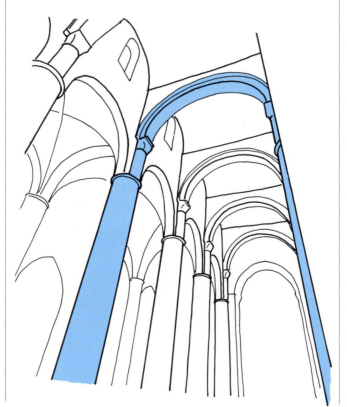

*Opposite page
Remains of Cluny abbey church. The huge new abbey church, founded in 1088, is 187 metres long and has a vast narthex, five aisles, a choir with an ambulatory and radiating chapels. It was almost completely demolished during the last years of the 18th century and the early decades of the 19th century. The few remains – the southern arm of the east transept and one of the towers – nonetheless give an idea of the impressive dimensions of the building, which became a model for numerous other ones in the region.*

The church
of Sant'Abbondio, Como.
Built in stone, the local
building material,
this shows the
characteristic motifs
of Lombard Romanesque
architecture, including
the blind arcades running
along the edge
of the gables. With five
aisles and a decorative
wooden roof, this building
has twin towers at the end
of the intermediary aisles,
reminiscent of solutions
in areas of Ottonian
influence, particularly
Germany.

Detail of the apse
of Sant'Abbondio, Como.

and aggregated, constitutes the entire organism. Most Romanesque buildings are simply a number of bays joined at the sides and arranged to form the plan. Further elements originated from the adoption of the bay. The cross resting on four piers is not, in itself, a stable form. It tends to "open," to push the piers outwards and, overturn them. The simplest way to overcome this problem is to place another identical bay beside it. In this way, the piers common to two bays receive two equal and opposing thrusts that cancel each other out, guaranteeing the equilibrium of the structure as a whole. The church can consist of a series of bays (usually square and arranged to form the plan of a cross) but only if the problems

Church of Sacra
di San Michele.
This is a highly unusual
building for its bold position
on the top of a mountain,
in Val di Susa,
and the successful contrast
between its massive base –
made of sturdy walls of gray
stone around spaces with
cross vaults sustained by
tall, strong piers – and the
lively decoration of its great
trefoil apse crowned by
galleries and built of green
serpentine.
The interior, of a later date,
already shows Gothic
features.

of three weak points
are resolved where the
bays end: the façade,
the east termination
and the sides of the
building. The simplest
solution is that of the
east end, where the
church usually ends in
one or more
semicircular niches
covered with a half-
dome: the apses. This
arched structure
successfully opposes
the outward thrust of
the series of bays.
The façade poses a
more complex
problem.
This is essentially a
flat wall containing
the building's
entrances. The thrust

Sacra di San Michele, detail
of the Zodiac Portal.

of the vaults could push the wall outward. There are many possible solutions to this problem and the Romanesque architects tested all of them. The simplest was greatly to enlarge the wall so that its thickness is a guarantee against all problems. A similar but far more refined and more common one is that using buttresses. When the terminal bay or bays of a church lean against the façade, they do not exercise the same pressure all over the wall, but only cause strain at the points where the piers would be in a normal bay. To eliminate the danger of collapse only these points need to be reinforced. This is done by resting large external piers against the wall of the façade; these must be thick enough not to be overturned by the thrust exercized upon them by the terminal bay. This solution is called the buttress and is one of the most obvious and characteristic features

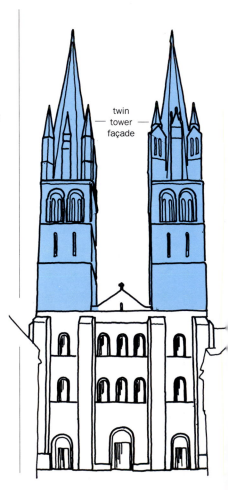

Abbey church of St-Nectaire, France.

Regional variations: France

France is a country rich in examples of Romanesque buildings and regional schools.
The most significant features include the twin-tower facade, developed in Normandy and then exported also to England. The church of St-Etienne in Caen, Normandy (left), is one of the finest examples.

twin tower façade

of Romanesque buildings.

As these buttresses are placed in line with the rows of piers inside, their presence on the façade also indirectly reveals the number of aisles in the church. More complicated solutions do exist and are sometimes used. Clearly, if two towers or a portico or even a number of apses, like those at the east end of the church, are placed against the façade, the system created automatically resolves the problem of thrust on that front.

Pilgrimage churches
The great pilgrimage routes passed through France and as a result a characteristic type of construction was developed in the Romanesque period that allowed several Masses to be said simultaneously in its many apsidal chapels. *In architectural terms it also lent great importance to the east end of the* building, as in the abbey church of Vézelay. *Generally, the large number of apses appeared in the form of radiating chapels (arranged on the radii of a circle around the axis of the church) set along an ambulatory, an aisle continuing the side aisles around the choir. On other, less frequent, occasions the various apses were arranged both around the ambulatory and along the transepts.*

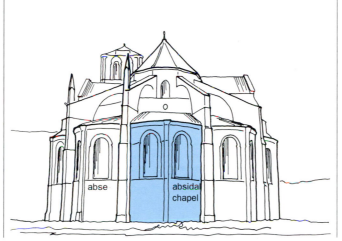

abse   absidal chapel

The last problem, posed by the side-walls, is more demanding and has a greater impact on the design. Again, there are several possible solutions. If the church just consists of a single aisle, that is the bays rest directly against the walls, the solution used for the front can be adopted again – either greatly thickening the wall or placing buttresses against it to absorb the thrust of the vaults. But churches with just a single aisle are the exception in Romanesque architecture.
The most typical form of church had three (or less frequently five) aisles: a central nave with the largest bays, and one (or two) smaller aisles on each side, also covered with vaults.
The inward thrust of the side vaults tends, of course, to counterbalance that of the central vaults. As the two vaults are not the same size (the side aisle is usually approximately half the

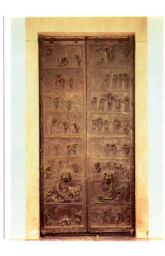

Bronze doors of the church of St. Michael, Hildesheim.

Regional variations: Germany
One of the characteristic German plans is that with a double choir, the central part being enclosed between two imposing apses.

The early 11th-century church of St. Michael, Hildesheim.
The model of the double choir is a more or less direct descendant of Carolingian architecture, but during the Romanesque period attained it great monumentality. Access to the church is from the side.

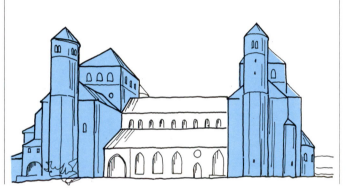

As well as the preference for buildings with a double choir, German Romanesque manifests a marked taste for complex articulation, especially concerning the towers, which become the dominant feature of the exterior. The same building may contain towers of every geometrical shape, as in this example of Maria Laach, a great Benedictine abbey at Nieder-Mendig, near Coblenz. It has an octagonal lantern tower and a central square tower (set back), two more slender round towers and, at the east end, two more square towers.

SECULAR ARCHITECTURE

The process of urbanization that marked the Romanesque period also had major consequences for secular architecture and town planning. It determined the initial expansion and sometimes transformation of ancient towns and the birth of the new villages that became the nucleus of many cities. Their original appearance has now been lost nearly everywhere, just as the secular architecture of the time disappeared with later changes. The ruins of many walls, crenellated and with round or square towers, and town gates, flanked or surmounted by sturdy towers, sometimes adorned with sculptures, do remain. Few towers of the nobility have survived; these were the residences of the most powerful families and usually consisted of simple, tall, massive quadrangular structures with smooth even walls or coarse rustication and very few windows. A number of these typical constructions, once the main characteristic of town skylines, survive in places such as San Gimignano and Corneto di Tarquinia, small villages that give an idea of what such great towns as Florence or Bologna, which numbered 150 and 180 towers respectively, must have looked like, although today they preserve but a few blocks of houses.

width of the central nave), there will be a residual thrust. This can be absorbed either by another, even smaller, side aisle, by slightly thickening the wall or by placing a number of buttresses against it. This system was used in various degrees in many churches of the

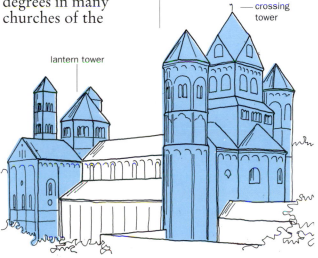

lantern tower

crossing tower

period. Two of the variations deserve particular mention for their importance. One is called "Lombard" (the major example is Sant'Ambrogio in Milan) and the other "Norman," as it developed, or reached its height, in Normandy and other countries conquered by the Normans, mainly England. Of the two the example of Sant'Ambrogio (perhaps the first church in Europe to use ribs to reinforce groin vaults) is visually the more attractive although conceptually it is more archaic. The solution adopted was to flank the nave (covered with large rib vaults resting on compound piers) with two smaller aisles, one on each side, covered with smaller and lower vaults. For every main bay there were two smaller bays between one compound pier and the next, the same

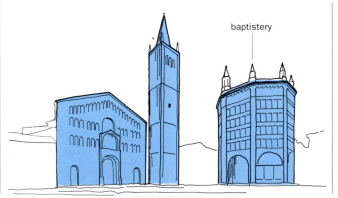

Façade of Trapani cathedral.

Regional variations: Italy

Italy is the exact opposite of Germany, manifesting a distinct preference for the physical separation of the various religious activities in different buildings. The typical Italian Romanesque model is that of one building for the rites of worship (the church), flanked by a bell tower and, opposite, almost with equal frequency a large baptistery (usually octagonal).

height as the piers. The whole was repeated in the upper story; the high part of the main bays was flanked by another aisle, constructed above the first and to the same dimensions and criteria. This was the gallery or tribune. The vaulted aisles and tribune balanced the thrust of the high vaults and their own thrust was easily contained by a fairly thick wall and small buttresses.

This often imitated and organic system, however, also caused some concern. First, if the central nave is flanked by structures

The cathedral and baptistery of Parma.
Another characteristic Italian Romanesque, as well as the typical screen façade with a gable and doorway preceded by a porch and tribune above, is the widespread use of the ornamental gallery, formed by rows of arcading.

of the same height, there is nowhere to put the windows. This explains why the Milanese church is illuminated only by the large windows on the façade. Second, as each main bay corresponds to two minor bays, a second pier stands between the main ones. This pier supports only the small vaults of the aisles and so is smaller than main ones, which must sustain a far greater weight. This means that to the spectator, the main

arcades look as if they are marked rhythmically by one large and one small pier alternately. In architectural manuals this rhythm is described as A a A a A. This accords with the spirit of the times which loved rhythm in the organization of its buildings. The second system, defined for brevity and convenience as Norman, is more refined. The general idea is the same but, instead of the tribune, sturdy buttresses are

placed against the piers of the main bays. This frees the upper part of the building to allow a clerestory to be introduced. This upper story pierced by windows rises above the aisle vaults. A second innovation also appeared – the cross vault was no longer divided into four parts but six, with a transversal rib added to the two diagonal ones. If extended to the ground like the others, this new rib falls on a smaller intermediary pier and

External view of the abbey of Sant'Antimo. One example of the penetration of influence from beyond the Alps to Tuscany is this Benedictine abbey, built in the middle of the 12th century. Its plan is divided into three aisles, with cross-shaped piers alternating with columns and an ambulatory with radiating chapels that links it to French culture, that of Cluny in particular.

Capitals of the nave
and central doorway
of San Michele, Pavia.

Facade of the church
of San Michele, Pavia.
Repeatedly rebuilt
and restored, San Michele
is a fine example
of a screen façade.
The upward movement
is accentuated
by the unusual position
of the windows,
concentrated in the central
area; the clustered shafts
of the buttresses dividing
the elevation in three,
and the row of galleries
converging toward the top
of the gable. The result
is a refined play
of chiaroscuro, enhanced
by the independent
sculptural decoration.

Nave of Ely cathedral. The Norman conquest led to the rapid construction in England of an incredibly large number of large abbey churches and cathedrals. Many of these were subjected to radical alterations in subsequent centuries. The interior of this church is marked by verticality and a lack of articulation of the aisle wall, likening it to those of Winchester, Norwich, Peterborough, and Durham.

makes it a compound one, the same as the others, giving the nave a far more accentuated rhythm (now an A A A sequence). The next style, Gothic, developed from this. This is the basic organization of the Romanesque church, the series of functions and related forms that make a "style" which, however, does not end with the elaboration of construction techniques. Added to these are a large number of decorative elements in an almost unlimited series of variations.

One of the main components of Romanesque architecture is the

Interior of the Panteón de los Reyes in the Collegiate church of San Isidoro, León. Decorated before the end of the 12th century, the vault has a series of frescoes depicting Christ in Majesty, apocalyptic motifs, gospel scenes of the infancy and Passion of Christ and the symbols of the months in medallions. The arches of the vaults rest on capitals, some with foliage and zoomorphic motifs, others showing examples of salvation from the Old and New Testaments which reveal great compositional confidence as well as a strong sense of volume.

arch, both a decorative and a functional element. This nearly always has a semicircular profile. Very often the arch is moulded, that is, accentuated with some degree of projection, or decorated with an alternation of light and dark colored stones or of stones and bricks dichromatism, a play – of light and dark that is one of the most picturesque and common decorative features in Romanesque art. Another half-functional and half-decorative characteristic is the rose window; this large circular, glazed window is the main ornament on the

Pisa cathedral is an example of the mainly decorative interest of Italian Romanesque. The treatment of the walls, especially the façades, is very unusual with the round arch and its supports used as an endlessly repeated module to obtain a three-dimensional effect.

Decorative features
The main and most commonly used decorative feature of Romanesque is arcading applied as an ornamental feature. This extreme example of Pisa cathedral is famous, the arcading being the basis for the design of the entire building.

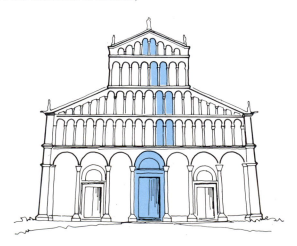

façade (and sometimes, although far less frequently, of the flanks of a church) and acts as a large highly decorated feature. The rose window is often the main source of light in the building, or at least in the nave. Another type of window called an "embrasure" came into fashion in the Romanesque period. Providing diffused

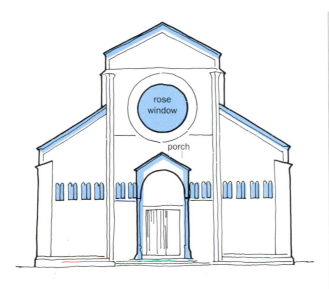

A common Romanesque feature was a gabled façade with the pitches of the aisle roof interrupted by a taller central element, showing that the nave is higher than the aisles. Equally common all over Europe was the rose window illuminating the nave. The porch raised on columns emphasized the doorway.

The façade of the church of San Zeno, Verona, conveys the internal division of the building into three aisles supported on columns and with a wooden roof. The extreme simplicity of the design is complemented by the decorative elements which emerge in the form of blind arcading, a large rose window, a porch resting on two lions and a continuous row of two-light windows accentuating the horizontal spread of the façade.

and subdued light while at the same time meeting safety and aesthetic considerations, this narrow slit opening set in the middle of a wall was splayed (progressively enlarged) toward the exterior (simple embrasure) or toward both inside and outside (double embrasure). Another

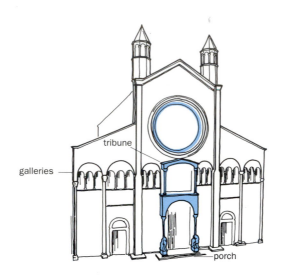

tribune

galleries

porch

Decorative features

The façade of Modena cathedral has, above the porch, a second niche that repeats the motif; this is the so-called tribune used to display relics on feast days. Also remarkable is the characteristic gallery that goes all round the building with arches grouped in threes under a larger one on supports that run down to the ground. This is another example of the use of the arch not merely as a structural feature but also for decoration.

Modena cathedral is one of the rare cases in which the name of the master builder is known: Lanfranco. This is one of the absolute masterpieces of Romanesque architecture. The church was designed to have a wooden roof. As a result the only thrust exercized by the arches on the walls is that of the main arcade on the façade wall. This is why two sturdy buttresses appear on the façade (and only on the façade) in line with the main arcade.

The abbey of Pomposa was consecrated in 1026 by Abbot Guido, a personal friend of the emperor Henry III and after his death honored as an "imperial" saint at Speyer. An atrium with a triple arch was added to the church.
The grandiose entrance, clearly in keeping with the pro-imperial ideals of the abbots, is matched by the large bell tower.

The bell tower of the abbey of Pomposa.
Despite considerable variety of form, Romanesque towers have some motifs in common. These include division into a number of tiered floors and the marking of the floors with windows, which increase progressively in size and importance as they climb up the building.

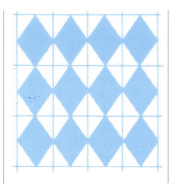

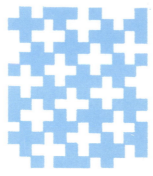

Interior of Notre-Dame-La Grande, Poitiers. The decorative element of many Romanesque buildings lies primarily in brightly painted geometric designs on the walls. It is rare to find a Romanesque church still in this condition, but many buildings in stone were originally conceived with similar effects.

Decorative features
Although many buildings of the period were constructed to exploit the decorative properties of stone or bricks, an important component of most Romanesque buildings was colored ornamentation, created with frescoes or mosaics. This decoration sought strong effects, bright colors and highly distinctive designs. Abundant on the walls of churches, it was sometimes also applied to other parts of the building, as in the case illustrated below.

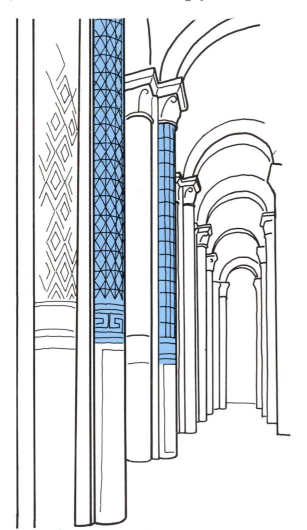

characteristic portal element appeared (especially in France) – the trumeau, a sculpted pier supporting the lintel and dividing the portal in two. The exterior was decorated with a number of motifs based on the arch: blind arcading, a typical Lombard feature, consisting of a band of small arches used as a decorative cornice beneath the

Interior of the Palatine Chapel, Palermo. Situated inside the Palazzo dei Normanni, this was consecrated in 1140 and dedicated to Saints Peter and Paul by Roger II. A true miracle of spatial and decorative harmony, it features the successful combination of a Byzantine centralized plan (presbytery) and a Latin basilica (nave). The beauty of the building is enhanced by the raised presbytery and the glittering mosaic floor with themes

inspired by Roger II. An example of the influence exercised by Byzantine theology in Sicily, the mosaics are set alongside elements of a pure Islamic-style, such as the wooden ceiling and the series of lively paintings depicting the pleasures of court life and the amusements of the prince, which are the largest Islamic painted cycle to have survived (regrettably retouched in the 15th century).

THE PILGRIMAGE ROUTES

During the 11th century the practice of making pilgrimages to sanctuaries that housed precious relics flourished and became a social phenomenon of vast importance. Safer roads and expanding towns greatly favoured this form of devotion. Unlike rich donations the pilgrimage was open to a far wider and more differentiated range of social classes. For Medieval man, as well as an act of penitence and propitiation, it represented the most effective way to secure the goodwill and protection of God and the saints. Moreover, especially in the case of long journeys to distant parts, it had the value of a fundamental experience, a sort of regeneration that left a profound mark on those who completed it. Many of Europe's sanctuaries were the object of pilgrimages but the main pilgrim routes led to the tomb of Christ in Jerusalem; to the tombs of Peter and Paul in Rome; and to that of the apostle James in Galicia, where, according to an ancient legends the bishop of Iria, guided by the appearance of a star (hence the name *campus stellae*), had miraculously discovered his burial place in 830.

Above
*The portals of the church
of St-Gilles du Gard.*

Below
*Capital with David and
musicians;
Jaca cathedral.*

Opposite page
*Doorway in the Pórtico de la
Gloria, Santiago de
Compostela.*

Decorative elements

In Romanesque churches
the portal was one of the
features that boasted the
greatest variety of
decorative solutions. A
typical one is the large
sculpted pier placed at the
center, dividing the entrance
opening. This element, a
point of contact between
sculpture and architecture,
was mainly used in France.

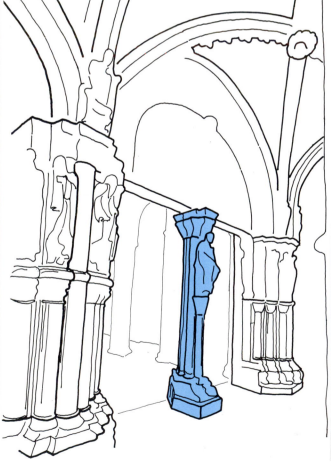

eaves or elsewhere; the gallery, that is, a number of arches united to form a band or a number of bands along the walls; and a characteristic porch, a small arched entrance in front of the church door, generally resting on two columns supported by crouching animals (usually lions).

As well as these mainly decorative details, there were variations in the plan of the building, depending on the different requirements and traditions in the various regions where the Romanesque developed.

Some of the most significant and most easily identified regional sub-styles can be mentioned in brief. France was of central importance, because its geographical position exposed it to many different influences and it had, at the time, the largest number of local models. In the north, in Normandy, a façade with twin towers – one

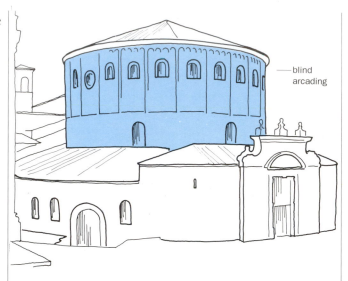

blind arcading

Round buildings

The classic Romanesque church is longitudinal but this does not mean that other kinds of buildings were not developed during the period. The case of buildings on circular plans is of particular interest. The Romanesque character is immediately apparent in the decoration and technique used for the wall. This example presents the characteristic band of blind arcading beneath the eaves, the splayed arches and bare masonry.

*Abbey church of St. Maria
Laach, Rhineland.*

Opposite page
*Most round churches are
in some way linked
to the preservation
of the relics of a saint
or martyr. The case
illustrated here
is an exception: Brescia
cathedral, a round church
erected for a large
community. This is the
finest example of a number
of buildings of this type that
mark eastern Lombardy.*

Right
*Baptistery of San Giovanni,
Florence.*

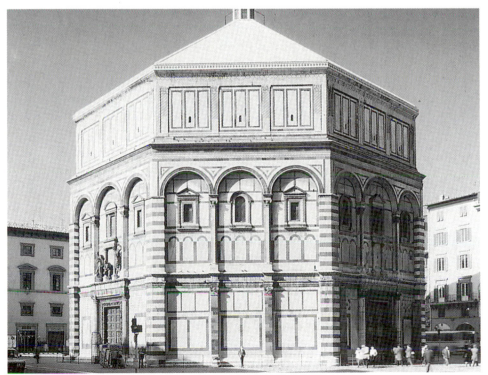

Rochester Castle, England.
Romanesque architecture
was not developed
for churches alone,
although they represent
the great majority
of the buildings that have
survived and are the most
typical of the style.
The Middle Ages was
the era of castles
and numerous examples
sprang up in every part
of Europe, conditioning
the landscape.

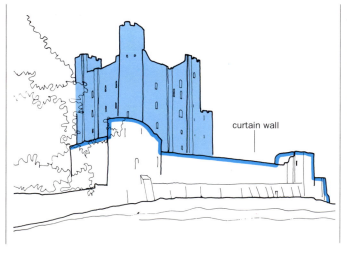

curtain wall

The castle and the palace
A number of characteristics
are peculiar to fortifications
erected in the Romanesque
period. One impressive
example is at Rochester,
surrounded by two rows of
walls reinforced at the
corners by towers.

France, the churches built along the great pilgrimage routes to the sanctuary of Santiago de Compostela were not completed with one apse, but with a more complex solution, making possible a complete tour of the eastern end of the church. To the three aisles of nave, transept, and apse were added apsidal chapels, most of them radiating from the great semicircular form of the apse. The most complex churches, however, were built in Germany.

Very often, they not only have some form of apse termination but repeat this on the other short side as well, thus enclosing the body of the church between two monumental terminations.

Moreover, it is typical of the German Romanesque to have a great number of towers, rising in various forms (square, octagonal, round) and with different dimensions both from the façade and from the apse or central part (in this last instance, a lantern tower that rises above the altar).

Unlike Germany, which combined all the religious elements in a single compound organism, Italy tended

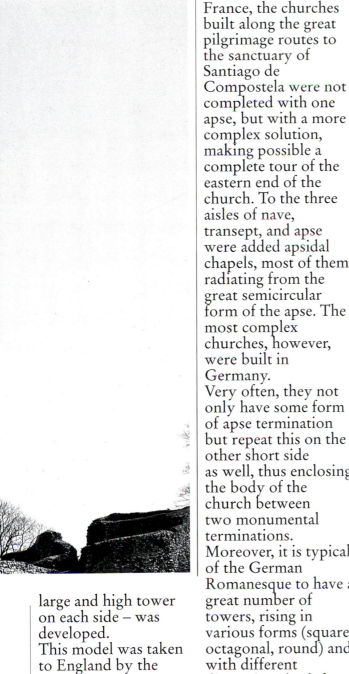

large and high tower on each side – was developed.

This model was taken to England by the Norman conquerors, where it became typical. Further south the groin vault was abandoned in favor of the more linear barrel vault, or a covering of Byzantine origin in which the groin vaults were replaced with as many domes. Also in

Palazzo di Anagni.
Examples of civil architecture of the Romanesque period are rare but they adopt the features typical of religious architecture, such as the arch motif.

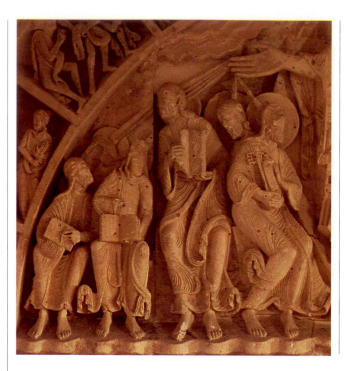

this is a wide chapel often placed at the east end of the building, almost a small separate church, and dedicated to the Virgin Mary.

In England the transept was also sometimes doubled, a design that became more common in the Gothic period.

It must also be noted that three elements appear very frequently practically everywhere and cannot therefore be attributed to any local school. The first is the

Architecture and sculpture
Although Romanesque sculptors possessed exceptionally inventive powers they were at the service of architecture and their work was principally used to decorate the main features of buildings. A decoration was never intended as an end in itself but for educational purposes, to instruct the onlookers. Even the compositional models had therefore to adapt to the architectural frame they were conceived for. Illustrated here is one of the most characteristic Romanesque portals.

to separate them. The typical Romanesque model for an Italian complex featured a number of individual buildings: the church itself; the baptistery, with a central plan and standing at the side or opposite the church; and the bell tower (usually flanking the church façade).

Simple forms prevailed for the church – a sloping screen façade or one with a gabled central section rising above the side parts. Above all, in the various regions, there were more decorative differences than structural ones. Rows of tiered arches appeared on façades in the areas of Pisa and Lucca, large colored marble inlays in the

Florentine buildings, Islamic decoration combined with Romanesque structural traditions in Sicily.

Other countries had fewer variations (though as many interesting examples) than the "three greats," England being an important example. Although many solutions of French origin were adopted here, these were not merely repeated but produced in original versions both in terms of building skill and, something that must not be undervalued, grandeur. The first rib vaults were almost certainly constructed in England, at Durham. The Lady chapel was also very popular in England;

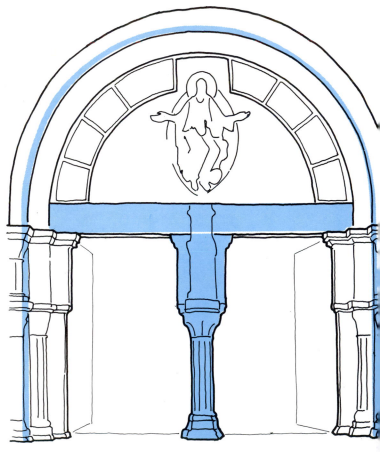

alternation of the piers, that is, the sequence of mayor and minor piers or of piers and columns, even when not justified by any particular constructional reasons, indeed even when there are no vaults to sustain. This can only be explained by the preference of the times for buildings with some form of marked rhythm. The second is the widespread presence of a crypt, small and generally covered with a groin vault, all or partially underground and situated beneath the main altar of the church, used to preserve the treasures and relics. Last is the existence, limited to a few important examples, of round churches – generally dedicated to the Redeemer and perhaps built on the model of the church of the Holy Sepulchre in Jerusalem. These represent an unusual interpretation of the Romanesque. Secular buildings have barely been mentioned although some do survive, though far fewer in number than the ecclesiastical ones. Most are castles and some are palaces. Actually, these buildings do not really correspond to the definition of Romanesque, which was coined mainly for religious architecture.

Doorway of the church of Ste-Madeleine, Vézelay, France.
The cycle of sculptures occupies two main areas in the architectural frame: the large trumeau supporting the lintel and the tympanum created in the semicircle above. Within this almost obligatory model – especially in France, Spain and England – the sculptor was free to organize the composition as desired around the central figure of Christ.

SCULPTURE

The various forms of art were not considered independent expressions in the Middle Ages. On the contrary, each was expected to make its contribution with the means available to the creation and decoration of what, alone, was considered the fundamental work – the building – the

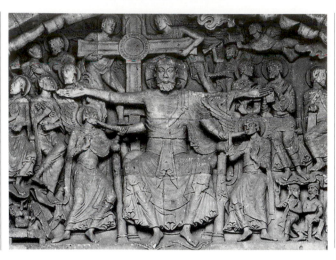

Left
Detail of the tympanum of the abbey church of Beaulien-sur-Dordogne.

Below
Tympanum of the portal of the abbey of St-Pierre, Moissac. The upper part contains a sculpted mandorla with Christ in Majesty and the lower part is divided into two horizontal registers, the first depicting figures and the other abstract designs.

The tympanum and lintel

The central position
of the tympanum (the upper
semicircle of the portal)
is usually reserved
for a figure of Christ
represented in glory;
this acts as the pivot
for the whole composition.
This subject is represented
in a majority of examples
within an unusual
and characteristic device
called a mandorla

– an almond-shaped "halo"
that is also found
in painting. This permits
both the unmistakable
identification of Christ
and detaches the figure from
the others crowded around
it. The lower part
of the tympanum and lintel
is often divided into one
or more horizontal registers,
filled with images of saints,
other repentant characters
or stylized designs.

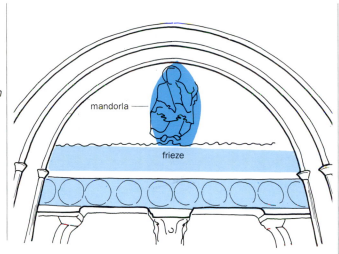

great church which the
community erected in
praise of its Creator.
Sculpture and painting
remained severely
subordinate to the
needs and preferences

of architecture. On the
other hand, this very
attitude meant that the
Romanesque building
was already conceived
as a fusion of
architectural parts in

the strict sense,
sculpted parts and
painted parts, and that
ample space was left
for sculpted or painted
decoration. Only some
buildings constructed

by monastic communities are an exception (such as the Cistercians whose rule "disapproved" of decoration). These buildings are almost totally devoid of sculpture or painting, their artistic content being entrusted to the bare architecture. In the rest, the great majority, sculpture was limited to certain parts, to the nodal, functional, or expressive points of the monument: doorways, capitals,

Above
*Frederick Barbarossa
and his entourage;
Milan, Castello Sforzesco.*

Stylization and repetition
*The stylization of figures
and their repetition
with minimal variations
are a typical feature*

of Romanesque sculpture.
*This reaches a height
in the frieze, in which
figures, carved in relief, are
arranged in a horizontal
band.*

Below
*Wiligelmo, reliefs portraying
scenes from Genesis;
Modena cathedral.*

*The Genesis scenes
become intense in tone
thanks to the remarkably
varied and expressive
gestures and poses of
these figures, which stand
out against the background
and reveal the personality
of one of Europe's leading
Romanesque sculptors.*

ambos (as the preachers' pulpits were called), corbels, mouldings and door surfaces. These parts were, in turn, conceived as true sculptural creations rather than as decorated architectural structures. The models implemented are extremely varied. Some of the most widespread features can, however, be summarized. The most characteristic feature is

Detail of the main doorway of San Marco, Venice. The decorative scheme consists of a mosaic lunette containing the Last Judgment, surrounded by three sculpted archivolts. As well as the usual prophets these also depict figures of sacred and secular virtues, allegories of the months, symbolic scenes of animals and putti and, lastly, a portrayal of the crafts, Venice having been the first of the Italian communes to organize these in guilds and confraternities.

the doorway and there can be one, at the entrance to the nave, or a number giving access to the side aisles and transept. The outline, save for very rare exceptions, is that of a rectangular lintel surmounted by a semicircular tympanum. The lintel is sometimes supported on a central, elaborately sculpted column between the two doors. The tympanum (or stone panel) is usually sculpted in some manner.

The doorway never opens flush with the wall, but is splayed to

Stylization and repetition
The model illustrated on page 56 also appears in this example, although with very different character. There are two types of image: human (in different poses but with a common imprint) and vegetable (small palm trees). These

are repeated rhythmically, lending order and structure to the whole. The principle, however, remains the same, the repetition of a stylized figure in horizontal rhythms.

Right
The door of San Ranieri at Pisa cathedral. Made in bronze by Bonanno Pisano and set in the right arm of the transept, this is a lively portrayal of stories from the life of Christ accompanied by some theophanic scenes.

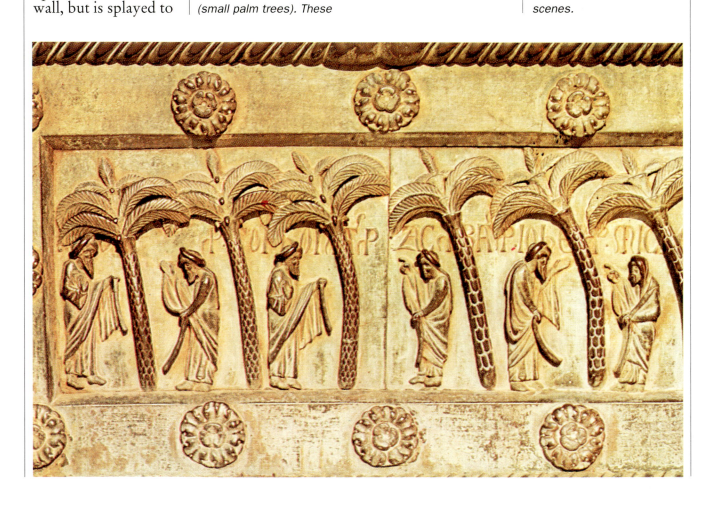

THEOPHANIC IMAGES IN TYMPANUMS

The decoration of portal tympana with monumental reliefs saw an early and vast development in the abbey churches and cathedrals of some French regions (Burgundy, Languedoc, Dordogne) and northern Spain. It spread more slowly and a sporadically in other parts of Romanesque Europe. For the worshipper, the image set in the tympanum of a doorway stresses the symbolic meaning of the "threshold," the passage from the space of everyday life to the holy space of the church. This, in its splendid architectural forms and ritual furnishing presents itself as the semblance of the celestial Jerusalem, the epitome of divine manifestation and revelation. By its very position, the image, therefore, is of an extremely theophanical nature (manifestation of the divine) and tends, at the same time, to become a vehicle of the overwhelming revelation of divine omnipotence, linked to the themes of universal redemption and the second coming of Christ at the end of time (parousia) to judge the world.

some degree; this means that although maintaining the same outline, it gradually slopes in from the outside toward the inside. Splaying is achieved technically using a sequence of sculpted bands, or orders. Generally speaking, the curving bands are decorated with geometric motifs, human figures or animals, or with an alternation of the two. The straight lower parts or embrasures are nearly always designed as small columns. The most significant and important part is the tympanum. There is nearly always a figure of Christ in Majesty at the center, larger in

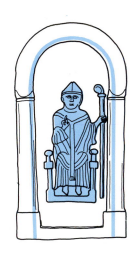

Sant'Ambrogio; Milan, Museo del Castello. The figure of the bishop, patron saint of the city of Milan is contained in a niche, with the most traditional of Romanesque architectural features, the round arch. This type of composition is repeated with remarkable frequency and seen in church niches (and their façades), stone tablets, and sacred ornaments, especially when there is a need to distinguish figures in a row from each other.

proportion to the other figures and enclosed in the typical "mandorla," a pointed oval that symbolizes divine glory. The lower part of the tympanum also nearly always contains one or two horizontal registers featuring fighting animals (a common symbolic representation of good and evil), processions of stylized characters or sometimes geometric motifs. This stylization and repetition of outlines or similar figures along a horizontal frieze is a typical feature of the

Above
Capital showing the Dream of the Magi; Autun, church of St-Lazare.

Left
Wellhead of Otto II in San Bartolomeo all'Isola. The use of the wellhead became widespread from the Roman period on. This is a parapet set around the mouth of a well and decorated in low relief.

Architectural models
Romanesque sculpture reveals its close links with architecture in many ways. The example illustrated on the left was produced in an almost endless number of variations. It shows a figure framed in a frieze, which symbolizes a building and sharply and neatly detaches the figure from those beside it.

A capital in Canterbury cathedral.
When decorated with sculptures, the back capital, with its four smooth sides, provided an excellent field for the portrayal of religious stories or the imaginary scenes peculiar to the Romanesque period. Compositions of this kind were not uncommon; here the forcefully expressive image is composed in a geometric X pattern.

sculpture of the period. It is presumably the result of a specific aesthetic choice, since the Romanesque sculptor was less interested in the individual and his physical characteristics than in the telling of a story. There is a typical preference for anecdotes, stories of everyday life and the representation of arts and crafts which sets it apart from the art of previous periods and from those that were to follow.

The second usually carved feature after the doorway is the capital. Unlike the period of antiquity and that from the Renaissance on, in the Romanesque period there was no standard form for this decorative architectural feature. There was a clear preference for capitals shaped like an overturned bell, but roughly square with rounded lower and side corners. The faces were used as panels on which to sculpt scenes from the Bible, pictures of tasks or of everyday life, fighting men or monsters, or

allegorical and invented figures. The Romanesque sculptural style ranged from the almost barbarically coarse, through brutal and lively expression to the realism and plasticity of Roman antiquity. Figures might be rendered in low or high relief. Some capitals are without decoration or have only simple geometric designs. A number of capitals, especially those that cap small columns in a cloister (a small enclosure with garden annexed to a church, typical of the Romanesque) often have an impost block, a sort of overturned truncated pyramid placed between the actual capital and the arch it supports. Doors are not always decorated. The material best suited to their sculpted

The block capital
The Romanesque period abandoned or transformed the details of the classical orders of Greece and Rome (Doric, Ionic, Corinthian, Composite). At the same time it elaborated a type of capital that became

peculiar to its style, the so-called block capital. This is the most common form of the Romanesque capital, that was used to support sculpted scenes (abstract motifs had been portrayed in classical antiquity).

This page
Capitals of the cloister of the monastery of Santo Domingo de Silos, Burgos.

The crucifix

Romanesque sculptors found the theme of the crucifix (which can be made of different materials) highly suited to their taste for intense and intricate ornamentation and to their love of animated, colorful and extremely expressive effects. They also liked compositions clearly inserted in a preordained structure, here the cross on which the Savior is placed. This is a very common representation in Romanesque art and its characteristics vary according to the country of origin. It is strongly expressive in Germany, solemn in Italy and stylized in Spain, where the Redeemer often appears fully clothed, the garments hanging in large flowing folds, often painted in bright colors. These Spanish works fully deserve their name of Majestades, Majesties, because the divine figure is presented more as a god in glory than a poor crucified man; some examples are also to be found in Italy and Germany.

decoration is bronze but the technical skill of working bronze was not equally common at the time in the various areas. When it was, the decoration is always based on the square with various panels depicting religious scenes, framed in turn with simple mouldings decorated with geometric reliefs and sometimes marked at the tops by lion's heads. These scenes may be replaced with single figures or wild animals. The composition is always very lively despite the simple and geometric pattern around it. Doors of this kind were widespread especially in the regions of central-eastern Europe: Italy, Germany, the Slav countries. Despite the subordination of sculpture to architecture, the Romanesque period was obviously far from opposed to a fusion of the two art forms. Very often sculpture stepped outside the areas traditionally assigned to it and, especially in the south (Catalonia, Provence,

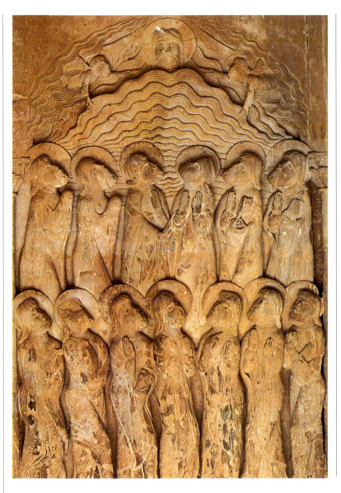

Italy) even covered the entire facade of a building, making use in this case of the frieze. This is a long, not very high, horizontal band divided from the rest of the surface by a decorated moulding that organizes the story told by the images. It is like a huge strip "cartoon," after all, the primary function of Romanesque sculpture was not to decorate but to "teach" the stories of the Bible to a very devout public that was unable to read. The frieze served this purpose very well. With their symbolism and allegorical structure, the scenes on portals, capitals and every decorated part of the building were conceived with this in mind. As far as the technique used to produce the sculptures is concerned; the Romanesque world had certain fundamental guidelines but there were huge variations in detail, depending on location, influence and era. General features were the total absence of any attempt to render the setting around the figures or the figures themselves in terms of reality. Varying degrees of deformation, symbolic transpositions and the mixing of real and imaginary aspects were the norm. The images were placed beside one another without being developed in depth.

Above
Ascension, *relief in the cloister of Santo Domingo de Silos, Burgos.*

Right
Deposition; *Volterra cathedral. Some fine surviving examples of wooden sculptures bear witness to the popularity of this art in the regions of central Italy in the 12th and 13th centuries. This beautiful Deposition exhibits affinities with the art of Benedetto Antelami, which was different from local sculpture, usually based on Lombard forms, but not lacking in Byzantine and some French influence.*

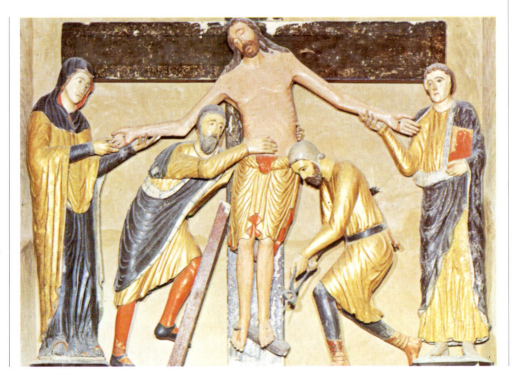

They simply fill the niches between one column and another or they are crowded on the surfaces of tympana and capitals in rhythmic, symbolic and expressive but not realistic compositions. The methods used to sculpt these figures are highly varied, from incised outlines to high relief with low relief dominating. The rendering of the images is sometimes unrefined and always distorted but lively and expressive to the highest degree. Romanesque sculpture may lack measure but never charm. Finally, the sculpture of the period does not appear in monumental examples alone, although these are the majority. There are numerous products of the goldsmith's art and other fine crafts, altarpieces, reliquaries and various religious objects, but a significant characteristic of the period is seen in the unusual crucifixes that the Spanish called (and still do) *Majestades*, or Majesties. These crucifixes on supports – sometimes simple and sometimes artistically worked – show Christ usually with very schematized clothing, as far more solemn than suffering (hence the name). This product, of which the prototypes were perhaps Italian, became common in the Mediterranean area with fine examples sometimes also being found in the north.

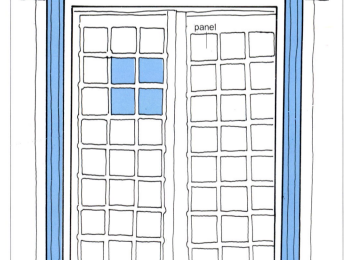

Bronze doors
The Romanesque Middle Ages saw a return of the technique of cast bronze in artistic works; there were no great statues as yet but bronze panels were applied to wooden doors. The scheme is simple and consists of dividing the two doors into squares, marked by geometrical divisions and possibly, as in this case, featuring lion heads at the top. One story was portrayed on each panel into which the door was divided.

Above
Barisano da Trani, bronze portal of Trani cathedral.

Opposite page
Portal of the church of San Zeno Maggiore, Verona. Doors of this type, divided into panels decorated with lively scenes, were more popular in the countries of central and eastern Romanesque Europe (Italy, Germany, the Slav countries) than in the West.

PAINTING

Unfortunately, many of the Romanesque achievements in the field of painting – frescoes, panels, and manuscript illuminations – have been lost. What remains may not even be the best of what existed, although it can be said with a fair degree of certainty that Romanesque painting was executed on every scale possible, not just on wood but also in the decoration of buildings and, at the other extreme, in very small illustrations on the letters and pages of manuscripts. In the first case, works were created in fresco (paintings applied over a fresh layer of plaster that absorbs the colors) or in mosaics, a form virtually exclusive to Italy, the country having the greatest contact with Byzantine culture. Mosaics were of particular importance in the finishing of interiors.

In the second case, there is a definitive art of tiny dimensions: the miniature or manuscript illumination.

Designs and techniques vary for these works, but less than would appear at first glance.

Themes are generally the same as those found in sculpture and also instruct by means of religious and historical pictures, portraying

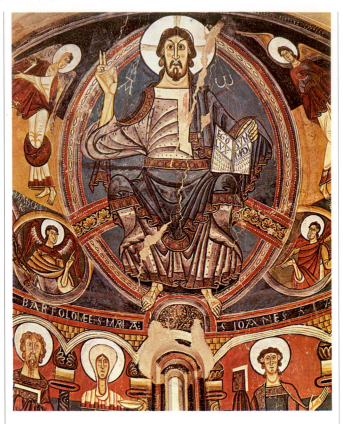

Christ in Majesty
A characteristic feature in Romanesque painting and sculpture was the mandorla, used to frame the representation of Christ in Majesty.
This page shows Christ in Majesty, from the San Clemente chapel at Tahull, in Catalonia; Barcelona, Museo de Arte de Cataluña. It is huge and visually dominated the interior of the church. The technique of harsh, essential lines with a great predominance of greens is typical of Catalan art. The bowl-shaped vault of the apse was an ideal position for the mandorla containing the representation of Christ.

Opposite page
Virgin and Child Enthroned, *from the church of Santa María at Tahull.*

episodes from the Old and New Testaments, the lives of the saints, human activities, epic events or past glories, everything that then came under the heading of *moralia*, stories with a moral content.

Second, the means of expression used are to some extent the same. Romanesque painting, like all the art of the period, was more concerned with effect than elegance and was more attentive to the content than to the decoration. Bright, even violent colors were often used and images may sometimes appear awkward but are always effectively expressive. As in the sculpture of the period, all canons or traditions that referred to the experiences of classical art were abandoned. Thus the artists no longer strove to render the background against which their characters moved realistically.

When they do hint at the natural or town environment in which their stories are set, this is done with symbolic means – a tree to signify

Above
Apocalyptic angels; Civate, Como, San Pietro al Monte.

Left
St. Liutwino, bishop of Treviri in the psalter of archbishop Egberto; Cividale, Museo Nazionale Archaeologico.

Models
The naturalistic representation of the human figure was not the ultimate aim of the Romanesque painter. The body is simply a support for the draperies, and the pose, sometimes agitated sometimes solemn, is never natural. Rigid compositional models prevail, often with stylized figure supports.

Detail of the frontal of the altar dedicated to St. Michael the Archangel; Barcelona, Museo de Arte de Cataluña.

As in the previous example, the composition is based on rigid models (despite the curves of the central cloth, which traces a curve of its own at the center of the painting, and the angels' wings). The model makes the story easier, as does the recourse to standard conventions such as the mandorla. Another very common one that appears here is the soul portrayed as a small infant which, having abandoned its body, is transported to heaven on a cloth by two angels. This may be a symbolic representation but was extremely clear to the medieval onlooker.

heaven on earth, a number of lines to indicate the sea and so on; nor are they preoccupied with the obvious unreality of what they draw.

Not only do they distort figures, this distortion is used to accentuate the expressive content, drawing attention to significant details, exaggerating poses to make situations clearer. They are aided in this by the highest sense of rhythm and stylization. Indeed the stylized composition, the rhythm created with repetitive patterns (many figures) always arranged equally, usually in a horizontal development, or symmetrically around

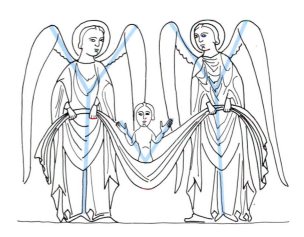

Left
The Last Supper, fresco on the vault of the Panteón de los Reyes; León, San Isidoro.

a central point of interest, is one of the most common and typical features of Romanesque works of art.

And while speaking of motifs it is appropriate to delve more deeply into the subject. As everyone knows, a painting is never composed by chance. It is always organized around a pattern of lines, masses or colors that constitute so to speak, the design of the painting.

These motifs can, more often than not, be represented with geometrical figures and this occurred in the Romanesque period too. But unlike those typical of other periods, Romanesque patterns, albeit simple and even direct, rarely make use of pure geometric forms:

Above
Interior of the basilica of Sant'Angelo in Formis.

Left
Mosaic showing St-Hilary; Venice, San Marco.
The treatment of the image is conceptually identical to that already observed for sculpture. However, Romanesque painting adds a sense of color, a detailed precision and an animation that are precluded from representations in stone.

The motifs
As well as angular, sharp-cornered designs Romanesque painting often uses an architectural motif to frame and separate figures. This is frequently in the form of the traditional arch on two columns.

triangles, pyramids, squares or circles. Nearly always the lines or curves are organized in groups of complex geometric forms. This type of painting is generally open in composition but stylized or at least strongly simplified in the figures. The colors may be very bright or more subdued but are always in an extremely varied range of shades. Indeed, critics use color differences and certain elements of design in order to distinguish one Romanesque "school" from another and to recognize the differences or similarities between different artists (usually unknown to us and identified only on the basis of their cycles of works; therefore we refer

PAINTED CROSSES

Monumental painted crosses, to be hung in churches at the end of the aisle or on the screen, were a typical invention of 12th century central Italian painting. The oldest, by Guglielmo, dates from 1138; later comes that of Lucca (in the picture) preserved in the Pinacoteca Civica of this town, and anonymous, but which is based on the first prototype. The shaped panel shows a crucifix with a large figure, surrounded by minor figures and scenes. Christ as Ruler of the World (*Pantocrator*) is at the top, the symbols of the evangelists at the ends of the arms and, where it widens at the center, are *St. John and the Holy Women*, *The Thieves* and *The Burial and the Resurrection of Christ*.

These crosses are not always attractive to look at. They lack drama (the iconographical type of Christ *patiens*, suffering or dead, imported from France and Byzantium, was yet to arrive in Italy) and show a provincial Byzantine style. Absent both from northern Europe and the eastern Mediterranean, they are nonetheless an important production, from which great masterpieces such as the *Crucifixes* by Giunta Pisano, Cimabue and Giotto descend.

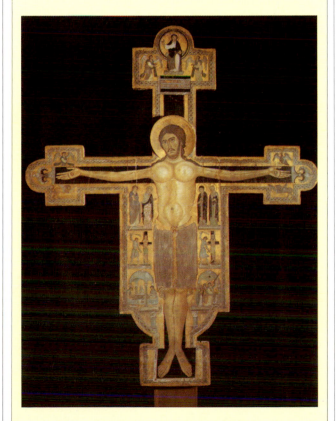

the "master of ...," referring to these cycles). The walls of the Romanesque churches that have survived are mainly bare but they were not always so. Often the intention was to cover the entire building or at least the main parts of it – the apse and the upper walls of the nave – with paintings. An almost obligatory theme for the decoration of the apse was Christ in Majesty in a mandorla; around the Redeemer was a symmetrical host of saints, men and the infernal powers crushed by Christ. This subject was often treated in different registers, each of which embraced an aspect of the story. Along the long walls of the nave ran a procession of saints or characters from the Bible; these also advance in large aligned figures or

The mosaic
The technique of mosaic decoration, numerous small tesserae in various shapes and colors combined to create a figure, was popular in Roman times, especially in the Mediterranean regions. These examples were more directly influenced by nearby Byzantine art, in which the mosaic was a decisive feature, not just in pictures but also to enhance architecture. The most fertile terrain for the art of mosaic was in those cities and regions in closest contact with Byzantium, such as Venice, which indeed developed its own Romanesque style, a mixture of the traditions of Constantinople and the new European achievements. This detail of a mosaic is

taken from San Marco in Venice. It is an example of a type of decoration that completes Romanesque architecture from the Veneto via Tuscany to Sicily.

The faces
Sant'Idefonso; Parma, Palatine Library. Romanesque art – so rich in conventions as to the situations to be represented – has no easily identifiable single general standard for portraying the human figure and facial expressions. Nor could there be one in an art spread over such a great time and space. Some lines are, however, common, such as the rendering of expressions, or at least the main features, solely with lines, indeed a conventional set of lines. There is a somewhat rounded rectangle for the

whole face, a single long line for the eyebrows and nose, a double line for the mouth and so forth. Of course, this general definition must be treated with due caution as methods and techniques changed from one country to another and from one master to another. It is, however, fairly valid especially for the more markedly European works.

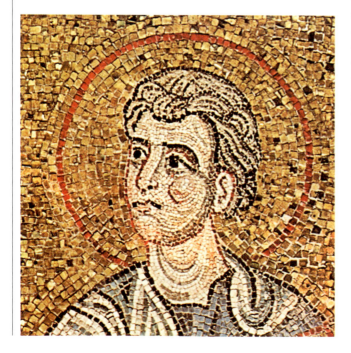

smaller images composed in tiered registers. In Italy, a country very close to (and greatly influenced by) the Byzantine world, the paintings are often replaced by large mosaics with a characteristic gilded background of Eastern origin. Less common than decoration with figures, but very characteristic of the period, is the decoration of the walls of the building (and especially the piers) with large and elaborate geometrical motifs. Last, Romanesque churches started to feature the first stained-glass windows, in bright colors; this was to become a fundamental feature of Gothic. In this period illumination was a truly

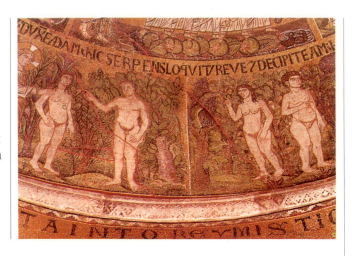

integral part of painting, such that patterns and influences of one activity were often taken up by the other. The field of book decoration is extremely vast but there are two frequent uses of illumination. One is the actual illustration of an episode, whether pertinent to the text or unrelated to it, but considered a suitable accessory for one reason or another; the other is the decoration of the initial letters of the chapters and paragraphs. Bright colors, imagination, the skillful condensation of long animated episodes in a small space and vivacious execution are the best features of this art. In every field the Romanesque was able to express itself consistently, and often brilliantly.

Left
Detail of the atrium of San Marco, Venice.

Right
Genesis *in the dome; San Marco, Venice.*

Gothic Art

Gothic art developed in Europe in the later Middle Ages (12th-14th centuries), at a time when profound economic and social changes resulted in the end of feudal society and the appearance of new centers of power – the first monarchies, cities, the clergy, and the "new" affluent classes of merchants and bankers. Although the economic and social framework within which this style flourished is clear, it is difficult to understand why art historians called it Gothic. This was certainly not because the Goths, a people who originated in Scandinavia, probably on the island of Gotland – were known as skilled architects; like all the barbarian tribes they were nomads, little interested in houses and, as pagans, even less so in churches. Nor was it because the Goths lived in the areas where this art form flourished, because in the 1st century B.C. they moved southward from the mouth of the River Vistula to settle on the left bank of the Danube. The word *Gothic* was probably

Opposite page
Detail of the ambulatory and radiating chapels of the abbey of St-Denis, completed in 1144.

Detail of the Tower of London, started in 1078 and subsequently enlarged. The Tower is a typical example of a castle-fortress; a curtain wall with thirteen towers protects the central block and is in turn surrounded by another wall with eight towers and a moat.

adopted by the Italian humanists of the Renaissance as a synonym for *barbarian*, in that it came from the regions north of the Alps.

Nevertheless, this art form called Gothic was born in the heart of France (which became a kingdom under the Capetian dynasty), in the fertile and prosperous area to the north of Paris known as the Ile-de-France, home of an excellent limestone that was durable and easily worked. Between 1140 and 1144 the choir of the abbey church of St-Denis, near Paris, was rebuilt by an unknown architect who can be regarded as the originator of the Gothic style. From this time onward, French cities vied with one another to build or rebuild their cathedral churches in this style: the facade of Chartres cathedral, Notre-Dame in Paris, the cathedrals, of Reims, Amiens, and Beauvais represent the height of French Gothic

architecture. From the Ile-de-France the style spread throughout Europe.

The French architect William of Sens started work on Canterbury cathedral, the first English Gothic building, in 1174; other masterpieces followed: Lincoln cathedral (begun in 1192), Wells cathedral, Westminster Abbey (1245), and Gloucester cathedral. German Gothic extended to the other German-speaking countries, Scandinavia and Eastern Europe, with masterpieces such as Cologne cathedral (where the first stone was laid in 1248), Freiburg cathedral, and the cathedral of St. Stephen in Vienna. In Spain and Italy, Gothic was less pure and lost its most distinctive characteristics.

Extremes were reached toward the end of the 15th century with so-called flamboyant Gothic, which, however, lacked the previous creative flair.

ARCHITECTURE

No specific date or event in 11th- and 12th-century European history marks the birth of the Gothic style but it should certainly be considered the product of a dynamic developing society that had broken away from feudalism. Numerous and diverse elements characterized this new European society. The new middle class of merchants and craftsmen lived in towns as free men and owed no allegiance to a feudal lord, although they were strictly divided into guilds and corporations. The centralization of power under strong kings in countries such as France and England meant that commercial activities were no longer disrupted by warring barons. As a result trade flourished and the growing cities

The west front of the cathedral of Notre-Dame in Chartres. The two towers flanking the façade give it height but differ in shape and proportion. The northern tower (on the left) was begun in 1134 and given a pierced, richly decorated spire in the early 16th century, bringing it to a height of 115 meters. The southern tower, begun in 1145, is 106 meters high; its spire alone measures 45 meters.

became aware of the influence they could now wield. The power of the clergy was also considerable, as bishops, abbots, priests, and monks increasingly attracted to power and material

possessions and in frequent conflict with the nobility, sought to extend their influence over worldly matters as well as the souls of their flocks. The Investiture Dispute between Church and

State over who should appoint bishops was a major cause of conflict during this period. Three main factors helped to produce the atmosphere in which the great Gothic cathedrals and

churches were built. There was a genuine desire to glorify God and proclaim the Christian faith. In the large cities the bishops and rich middle classes, safe behind strong walls, felt a

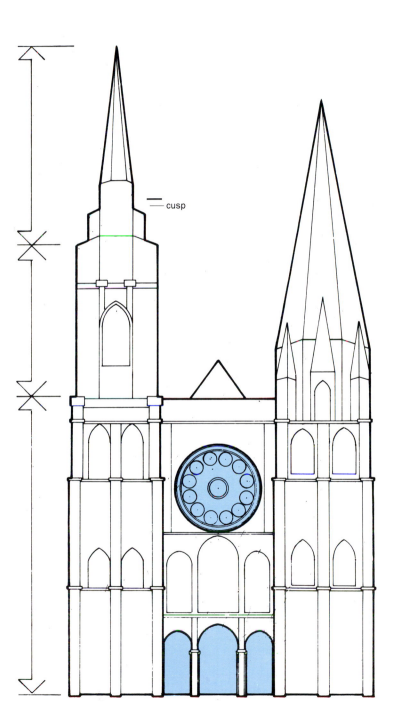

cusp

The façade
Chartres cathedral contains many features typical of Gothic architecture: portals on the outside conveying the fact that the central nave is higher than the aisles; a large rose window; and soaring towers bound to the façade by precise proportions (for example the spire of the left-hand tower is equal to approximately one third of the total height; the section below it is half the height of the façade).

justifiable pride in "astonishing and enchanting" the world with immense cathedrals that towered above the houses and could be seen for miles around. And the medieval philosophy of scholasticism taught that it was not only possible to reach God through faith but also through reason. God could be reached through the exercise of complex but refined thought, rigidly formal yet rich in subtlety. These precepts inspired the architecture of the Gothic cathedral, reaching up toward God with complex but refined structures, rigid in form but rich in detail. The soaring visual effect reveals the transformation of taste, philosophy and aesthetic ideals implemented in architecture with the introduction of several original elements that are typical of the Gothic style: the pointed rib vault, the use of pointed instead of round arches and

The central portal, known as that of the Last Judgement, *on the main façade of Notre Dame in Paris is a typical example of the harmonious blend of Gothic architecture and sculpture. It is divided into a number of deep embrasures cut obliquely into the thickness of the masonry and entirely covered with sculpture. The archivolts are decorated with angels and saints from the Celestial Court; the bases feature the Virtues and Vices.*

The tympanum

Built around 1220, the whole portal is named after the figures carved on the tympanum; the center is dominated by an image of Christ the Judge seated between Mary, St. John, and angels bearing the symbols of the Passion. Virtually all the available space is filled with sculpted decoration, as is normally the case in Gothic portals. The central pillar, or trumeau, also bears a carved statue.

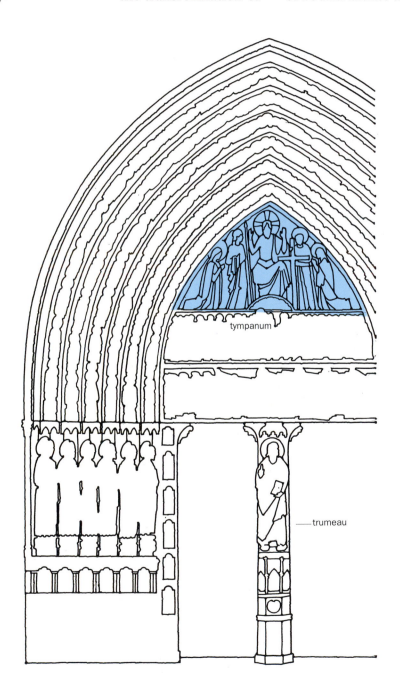

tympanum

trumeau

The apse of the cathedral of Notre-Dame in Paris begun in 1163 and completed in the 13th century. A lovely play of lines is created by the slender flying buttresses needed to carry the lateral thrust of the vaults down to the ground.

Flying buttresses ...
The apparently light flying buttresses of Gothic cathedrals serve a specific structural function, transferring the lateral thrust of the pointed rib vaults to the buttresses and then to the ground.

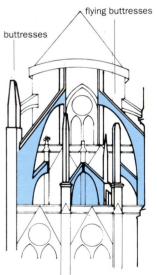

buttresses flying buttresses

flying buttresses.
To recognize a cross vault, imagine two cylindrical corks each cut in half lengthwise and set on a table. Each half represents a tunnel or barrel vault and, when arranged in the form of a cross, a cross vault. Place the four half corks to form an X or the arms of a cross. You will see that they can only be joined if their ends are sharpened to a point. This makes a cross vault. The four intersecting parts are called the webs of the vault; the structures that take the weight of the vault and intersect to form an X, dividing the vault into the four webs, are called ribs and converge on the highest point of the vault, known as the keystone.
Gothic architects were obsessed with gaining height and could not be content with the cross or groin vault.

...and buttresses

Detail of the cathedral of Notre-Dame in Chartres. The flying buttresses link the main body of the building to the external support of the buttresses, which reinforce the wall, and counter the thrust transmitted to it.

They needed a more pointed structure, one that reached upwards. An unknown master builder – as architects were called at that time – invented the pointed cross vault. This was obtained by bringing the four piers supporting the vault closer to one another and changing the semi-circular arches into pointed arches; the ribs are also pointed and the keystone is at a higher point than in the normal cross vault. There is a great advantage in the pointed cross vault: it is solid, elastic and light as the weight of the webs is discharged on the ribs which convey it to the four points of support, the piers or columns. A pointed vault however presents some static problems. Because of its pointed-shape and its height, it not only exercises downward thrust – absorbed as we have seen by piers or columns – but also a strong side thrust, neutralized with the use of large flying buttresses; these are half arches that serve as lateral supports for the vault. They are frequently used over the roof of the side aisles to counterbalance the thrust produced by the often very high vaults of the nave and to carry it to sturdy buttresses on the outside of the walls. With this original building method, the weight of all the architectural elements is discharged gradually (starting from the highest point of the church, namely the keystone of the nave)

Essential design

The absence of decoration highlights the Gothic framework of the Prague synagogue. The transverse arch that defines the cross vault and the ribs that take its weight and divide it into cells rise from the capitals of the responds on the walls.

Interior of the lower church of San Francesco at Assisi. Although it had to respond to various requirements, the church of San Francesco at Assisi was initially built as the burial place of the Order's founder. By tradition a saint's tomb was placed in a crypt but here the crypt was made as large as a church. Two churches were built one on top of the other, the lower a crypt-church and the upper, a church used for preaching, central to Franciscan teaching.

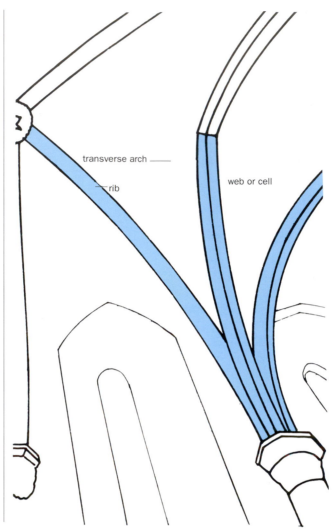

transverse arch ⎯⎯

⎯ rib

web or cell

from the inside outward down to the ground. All these structures, the high, slender arches, piers and ribs, seem to defy gravity, rising to fantastically giddy heights; this gives the worshiper a sense of the remoteness of heavenly transcendence, heightened by the fact that those inside the cathedral cannot grasp the laws of construction that govern the whole. The technique employed to sustain the vault – flying buttresses – can be understood only from the outside. These seemingly miraculous structures are perhaps just that if you consider the difficulties and sacrifices endured by the people of Reims, Chartres, Paris, Amiens, Beauvais, and so many other towns and cities in France and throughout Europe to construct these splendid "hymns to God." Anonymous donations made by thousands of affluent citizens and the voluntary labor offered are just some examples of the general commitment required to build these impressive churches. The people of Chartres even took the place of the exhausted horses and themselves pushed carts of building materials through the narrow streets to the elevated cathedral site. The Gothic cathedral interior was in the shape of a Latin cross, running from east to west according to religious symbolism, with the altar placed at the east side, "with the rising sun." Three aisles divided it, the central nave higher and wider than the other two aisles. Occasionally it had five aisles. The shorter part of the cross, the transept, was usually divided into three aisles and protruded slightly from the main longitudinal body of the cathedral. Characteristically, the exteriors of Gothic transepts have monumental façades, often, like the west

Left

Detail of the vaults of the Prague synagogue, built in or around 1270. For its economy of form and the absence of decoration this building is one of the purest examples of Gothic architecture and resembles the interiors of certain abbeys and monasteries.

Left

The nave of the cathedral of St-Etienne, Auxerre.

front, framed by towers and enriched with large doorways. Chartres cathedral, for instance, has nine doorways, three on the main façade (including the famous Royal Portal, left miraculously intact after a disastrous fire in 1194) and three, half concealed by splendid sculpted arches, on the east and west transept façades. In the choir of Gothic cathedrals the aisles extend beyond the transepts to form a wide corridor, called the ambulatory, behind the main altar. The grandeur of the choir is also enhanced by a number of chapels set around the ambulatory. The nave is separated from the aisles by rows of pointed arches resting on slender clustered piers and half-columns. The piers are quite close together and this is another original innovation of Gothic architecture. Previously, the bay, that is, the space circumscribed by four piers and the cross vault connecting them, was square. In Gothic cathedrals the architects divided the space of a square bay into two rectangular

Above
Interior of the church of Santa Maria Novella, Florence.

Left
Interior of Orvieto cathedral. The round arches along the nave are very wide, an effect heightened by the use of long arcades, cornices and a two-color decoration all over the piers and walls. A striking contrast is produced between the spatial movement created by chiaroscuro below the cornice and the simplicity of the walls above it.

Opposite page
Interior of Cistercian abbey of Fossanova, Lazio.

Main elevation of Cologne cathedral. The clustered piers bears statues of the apostles beneath canopies. The piers are clearly the wall's only forms of support, with the arches, triforium and stained-glass windows merely separating it from the aisles, low down, and from the exterior, above.

Light walls

The walls of the great Gothic cathedrals have no structural function so the masonry could be reduced to a bare minimum. The nave was defined at the bottom by pointed arches and at the top by a triforium (a gallery of arches resting on slender supports) and clerestory containing large windows.

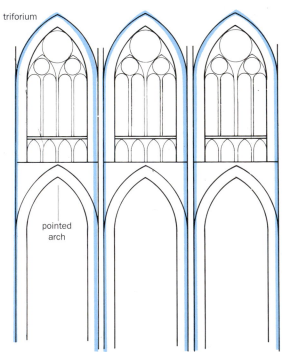

triforium

pointed arch

bays, in which the short side of the rectangle corresponds to approximately half the side of the existing square. The number of piers is thus doubled, and the smaller distance between them brings two advantages: each pier has to support a far smaller thrust (practically half) and it is possible to build pointed arches and vaults which, as we have seen, lend greater height to the construction. When you enter a Gothic cathedral you have a breathtaking sensation of height. This effect is due in part to the actual height of the nave (that of Notre-Dame in Paris is 35 meters high, that of Reims 38 meters and of Amiens 42 meters) and partly to the height-width ratio, the latter invariably being very limited. The ratio of Chartres cathedral is 1:26, that of Notre-Dame in Paris 1:2.75 and that of Cologne cathedral 1:3.8. This soaring verticality was in some cases the undoing of the architect, as in the choir of the cathedral of St-Pierre at Beauvais (completed in 1272); its vaults were erected at a record height of 47.5 meters only to collapse in 1284. As the Gothic method of construction allowed the vertical weight of the vaults to fall only on the piers and the side thrust on the flying buttresses (anchored directly to the ground on the outside of the building), the walls no longer served as supports and could safely be filled with large windows and arches. The exclusively Gothic invention of pierced walls freed them from their sense of mass to become a light partition of multicolored glass. If the walls were removed from a Gothic building, the skeleton of piers, vault ribbing and flying buttresses would remain intact – just like modern reinforced concrete constructions. The walls almost disappear; indeed from the inside of a church they are scarcely noticeable.

Above
Detail of the interior of the Dominican church of Jacobins at Toulouse.

Left
The nave of the church of St. Elizabeth in Marburg. Pointed arches and vaults have been used systematically to create a hall church with aisles of equal height that converge on an east end on a trefoil plan, a design typical of the Rhineland.

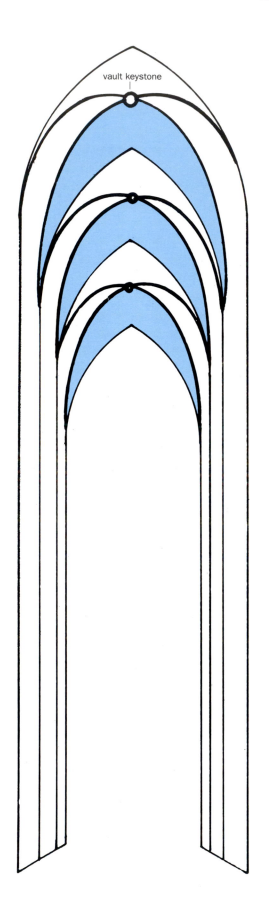

vault keystone

Slender piers with pointed arches flank the central nave; above these, is a small gallery or triforium, overlooking the central nave through pointed arches (usually divided into three, hence the name) and resting on slender columns. Frequently, as in Cologne cathedral, the triforium is above the roof of the aisles, its outer wall pierced to provide extra light. The upper parts of the church have huge stained-glass windows decorated with figures.

These windows usually have two lights (that is, they are divided into two pointed arches by slender columns). The top of each window is pierced with a circle at the center, usually multifoiled.

These stained-glass windows are brightly colored, with a predominance of ruby red, violet, and emerald green. The light filtered through the windows into the interior of the church seems not to come from a natural source and produces a warm, bright atmosphere, instilling a sense of ecstasy in the worshiper. These decorated windows were not invented just to bring light into the churches; as one medieval monk put it, they also showed "simple people unfamiliar with the Scriptures what they should believe." The Bible stories in pictures taught an illiterate population Christian doctrine and religious truth, rather like the modern-day comic strip or color

The choir of Cologne cathedral, begun in 1248. The elongated, vertical proportions of the interior of this cathedral generate a strong sense of mysticism. The impression of height is further accentuated by the vertical clustered piers and the absence of interruptions made by horizontal elements such as capitals or protruding cornices.

Mystical height
The exceptional soaring effect of the choir of Cologne cathedral is increased by a height-width ratio of 1:3.8, a record for Gothic cathedrals. The drawing also highlights the way the ribs converge on the highest point of the vault, known as the keystone.

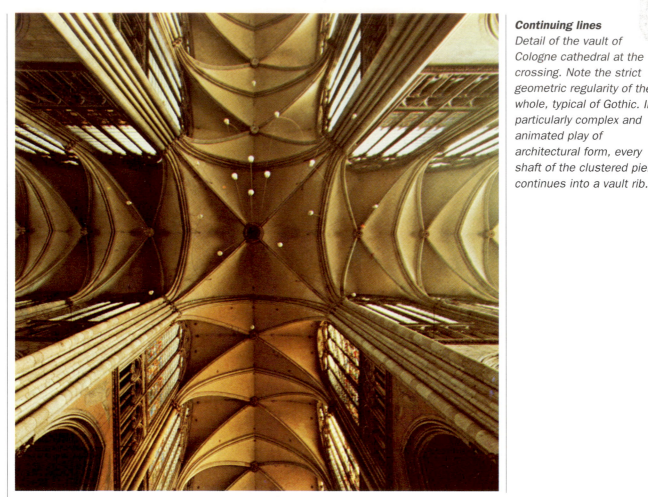

Continuing lines
Detail of the vault of Cologne cathedral at the crossing. Note the strict geometric regularity of the whole, typical of Gothic. In a particularly complex and animated play of architectural form, every shaft of the clustered piers continues into a vault rib.

illustrations in books. The transparent stained glass heightened the effect of the stories told, because for the medieval Christian – recall St. Francis and his praise of the Lord – light, as all the other gifts of Nature, came directly from God. The exterior of a Gothic cathedral reflected the interior and featured the same soaring verticality and lightness of structure, reaching up towards the sky. These effects were obtained on the façade by playing down all horizontal lines and shapes and enhancing the vertical ones. The compact external walls were broken up by a series of portals, windows, rose windows, arches and statues so that the voids predominated, giving the desired sense of ethereal lightness. Towers on either side of the façade reinforced the impression of an upward surge. This feature is constantly seen on the cathedrals of the Ile-de-France,

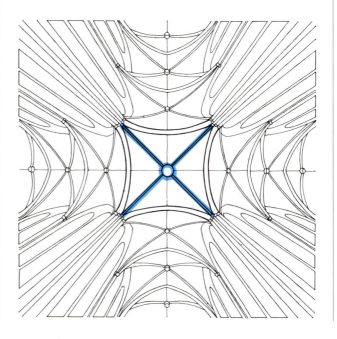

the birthplace of the Gothic style. These towers have large apertures level with the bells and usually terminate in cone-shaped or pyramidal spires – slender, pointed silhouettes that seem to draw the entire building upward. The facade of Chartres cathedral, a typical example of these architectural principles, is divided into three levels by horizontal cornices; at ground level three splayed portals set in the thickness of the wall are richly decorated with friezes and sculpture. Three large windows on the central level light the interior and the top level is dominated by a rose window. The central doorway and corresponding window are taller than those on either side, almost as if to stress the greater height of the nave inside on the exterior. The buttresses set against the stonework

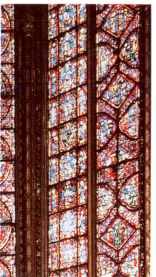

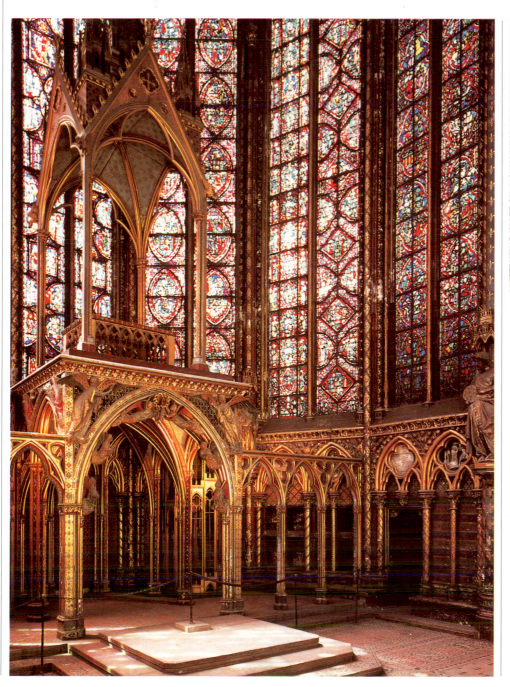

The chapel of the Palais de Justice in Paris, Ste-Chapelle was erected for St. Louis, king of France, as a palace chapel and to house precious relics brought from Byzantium. The walls are virtually abolished and replaced with decorated stained-glass windows, separated by slender composite piers.

One of the 176 windows in Chartres cathedral. The vertical arrangement of the scenes lends upward height. The sunlight passes through the brightly colored glass windows depicting scenes and stories from the Bible and illuminates the interior of the church to remarkable effect.

Tracery

This four-light window in Notre-Dame in Chartres is divided by moulded mullions that terminate in trefoil pointed arches; the upper part is formed of elaborate geometric tracery of rhombuses and multifoiled arches.

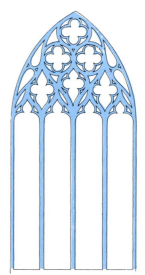

between the portals and windows also reproduce the internal divisions on the outside. They have another purely aesthetic purpose: their vertical lines counter the horizontal lines of the cornices separating one level from another to restore a perfect balance.

The upper part of the façade is dominated by a large rose window, a major and characteristic feature of Gothic architecture. The circular shape, divided by narrow ribs of stone like the spokes of a wheel, had, for the Christian of the period, two symbolic meanings, alluding simultaneously to the sun, the symbol of Christ, and the rose, that of the Virgin Mary.

It also served a dual function: it was an additional source of light (the rays of the afternoon sun, filtered and colored by the stained glass, sometimes pass through the rose window to the main altar, producing spectacular effects), and it gives its wall (the only "visible" one, the others being a play of arches and windows) a sense of lightness with its elegant lacelike tracery.

LIGHT IN GOTHIC ART

Light played a new and fundamental role in the new religious buildings. Gothic architects perfected a system of piers and vaults that would allow them to replace walls with large windows and create "diaphanous" structures. Daylight flowed into the churches to great effect, its rays illuminating aisles, ambulatories and transepts and reflecting off the shiny surfaces of the gold and silver altar furnishings. "When the new rear part is connected to the front" wrote Abbot Suger, about to rebuild the nave of St. Denis after having already done the choir (in the picture), "the whole church will be lit up by the bright central area. Luminous is what is luminously combined with the luminous. And luminous is a fine building flooded with new light." Such was his desire for light that Suger seems dazzled by the project and repeatedly juxtposes the words "light" and "luminous." The emphasis of the sentence well renders the supreme value that the abbot and his contemporaries attributed to luminosity, as to introduce innovatory building techniques that would dispel the shadows of Romanesque churches and create a new architectural model. The appreciation of light is a central and recurring theme in the religious culture of the 12th- and 13th-centuries. Thomas of Aquinas and Hugh of St. Victor, theologians, identified beauty with harmony of proportion but also with luminosity: "What is lovelier than light," writes Hugh of St. Victor, that which, although devoid of color, illuminates and reveals the color of things?" The beauty of light is strictly linked with its metaphysics, with the idea, already stated in the Gospel according to St. John and in the writings of St. Augustine but developed mainly in the works of a neoplatonic Christian of the 5th century A.D. called Dionysius the Areopagite, that God is light and creation was an act of illumination. (In the photograph: window in the left transept of Chartres cathedral).

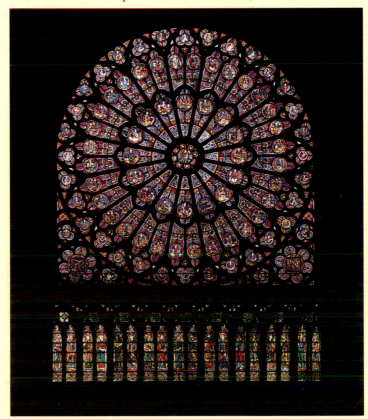

Pure geometry

An external view of the rose window on the west front of the cathedral of Notre-Dame in Chartres. The structure consists of three concentric circles and corresponds to precise geometric criteria.

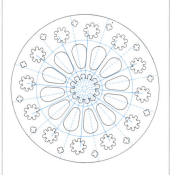

The rose window in the west front of Chartres cathedral seen from the inside. The geometric structure of the rose is clearly visible from the outside whereas the inside view reveals the splendor of the multicolored glass that filters the light. It was made between 1210 and 1220, during rebuilding work carried out on the cathedral after the disastrous fire of 1194.

The west front usually features a gallery of pointed arches on slender columns and containing a number of niches, each housing a statue. This lightens the appearance of the stonework and connects the two towers flanking the façade.
Thanks to the presence of the flying buttresses, it is the exterior and apse of a large Gothic cathedral that most reveal the building's structure.

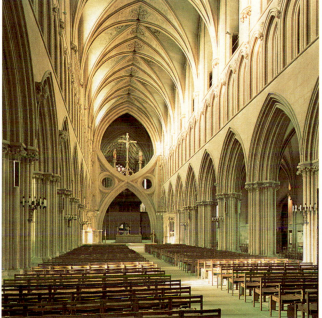

The façade of Wells cathedral in England was built between 1230 and 1240. This homogeneous screen of niches, pointed arches and buttresses harmonizes the internal division of three aisles. Verticality is countered by the high base with three small portals and the string-course moulding. A reinforcing structure with opposing pointed arches was added inside to sustain the nave after the erection of a huge tower above the crossing transept in or around 1340.

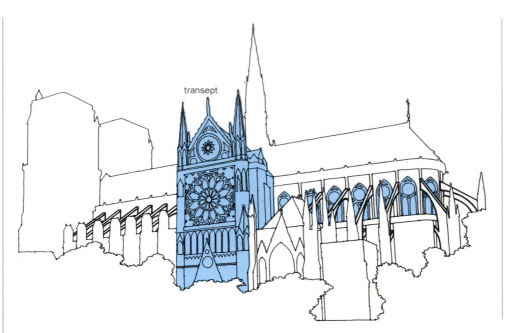

transept

The transept
The development of the transept – the transverse arms of a cross-shaped church – is a common feature of Gothic cathedrals. Often it is divided into aisles and its monumental façades decorated with large portals, statues, arcading and rose windows.

However, the architectural features typical of Gothic (spires, pinnacles, statues and sculptures) bring the elevation that symbolizes man's reaching up to the sky to these parts as well. Because its vaults are so high, the nave has a steeply sloping roof. Flying buttresses set slanting or perpendicular to the external wall of the cathedral join its highest part to the other buttresses and the roofs of the aisles. Sometimes there are two or more rows (orders) of flying buttresses, disguised by tall pinnacles rather like miniature towers or spires decorated with carvings, usually of leaves, flowers and so on. The spires and pinnacles, again typical of Gothic architecture, have no specific constructional function (if not to weigh down the buttress) and merely emphasize the sense of height and lighten the appearance of the building. A groove was cut into the top of the uppermost flying buttress to carry rainwater down from the roof of the nave into imaginatively carved spouts known as gargoyles.

A last unusual feature of large Gothic churches is the close link between the architecture and the sculpture, whether large statues, pinnacles-reliefs, ornamental spires, pillars, or buttresses. Religious subjects inspire most of the sculpted images, and they seem to turn the cathedral into a great

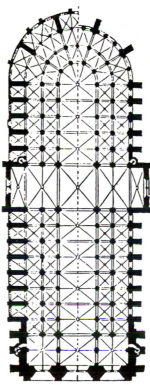

illustrated encyclopedia of figures carved in stone that condenses the knowledge of all time. Religious themes from both the Old and New Testaments include saints and prophets with their identifying symbols – St. Peter with his keys, St. Barbara with her tower, St. Margaret and the dragon, Jonah and the whale – as well as narrative cycles such as the Last Judgment, the crucial moment in the life of a Christian, usually placed over the central

Above
The south side of the cathedral of Notre-Dame in Paris. The transept was begun by Jean de Chelles in 1258 and completed around 1270. Its façade is extensively pierced and light, with two rose windows one above the other, the larger having a diameter of approximately 13 meters.

Left
Plan of Notre-Dame.

doorway of the west front.

The seven liberal arts were a favorite profane subject: Grammar was symbolized with a small whip; Rhetoric with a book; Logic with hair enclosed in rings, or sometimes a scorpion or serpent; Arithmetic with an abacus; Geometry with a compass or plumb line; Astronomy with a sphere or sextant; Music with a lute. The months of the year were often represented in terms of seasonal agricultural tasks, the signs of the zodiac, and even historical events. Sometimes

Above and left
Lorenzo Maitani, Hell;
details of the reliefs of the
Last Judgment on the fourth
buttress of the façade of
Orvieto cathedral. Maitani
was a sculptor of delicate
lyricism or intense emotion,
as demonstrated by the
dramatic figures of the
damned seized by the
fearsome devils of the
inferno.

Opposite page
The Pillar of Angels,
Strasbourg cathedral.

there are direct references to the contemporary world as in the "gallery of kings," portraying the French monarchs from Charlemagne onward, seen in numerous French cathedrals. The statues seen on the exterior of a Gothic cathedral adopt the same principles of soaring verticality that inspired its architecture. The stance is rigid, with the arms close to the body, legs straight, and feet dangling. Shoulders and hips are unmarked and the folds of the garments fall in rigid parallel

Master of the Months, September; Museo del Duomo, Ferrara.

The gallery

Galleries containing statues of sovereigns or saints are typical of Gothic churches. Here, pointed arches resting on columns create a gallery containing statues integrated in perfect proportions. Although the poses are similar, the gestures of the statues differ slightly.

lines, almost like the flutes of a column, to accentuate the height of the figure. The heads were usually small in proportion to the bodies and the faces express spirituality and beatitude, emphasized by elongated eyes and fine, gently smiling lips. The figures are bound to the architecture by an overhead canopy and a carved base, which forms a sort of niche. Another decorative feature of Gothic architecture was the ornamentation of the portals. These were cut in numerous deep embrasures, splayed

Master of the Months; January; Museo del Duomo, Ferrara.

Left
This gallery containing statues of kings is on the south side of Chartres cathedral. It is a classic example of the bond between Gothic architecture and sculpture, the pointed arches and slender statues satisfying the aesthetic canons of upward tension that inspired the construction.

into the thickness of the wall. The lower part of each embrasure contained a statue, while the upper part, corresponding to the archivolts (the mouldings which follow the contour of an arch), was carved with a series of reliefs or statuettes. The central pillar, or

trumeau, dividing the doorway also contained a statue. The decorative carvings around the portals were inspired by nature: rose and strawberry bushes, ferns, vines, oak and maple leaves, all executed with great refinement.

Although the great

cathedrals were probably the finest achievements of Gothic architects, they did not work only for bishops and rich cities seeking to glorify God by erecting new churches. They often undertook commissions for the monastic orders, particularly the

canopy —

pedestal —

Opposite page
Column figures sculpted between 1200 and 1215 adorn the central doorway of the south transept of Notre-Dame cathedral in Chartres.

Column statues
Those of Chartres cathedral are a typical example of column statues. Figures of saints and prophets set against a column; although detached in high relief they are closely linked to the architecture, helping both to lighten the structure and accentuate the upward movement. The figured pedestal and multifoiled canopy further stress the bond between the statues and the architecture of the cathedral, which frame each figure. Despite the apparent uniformity, there are slight variations in the gestures and facial expressions; the second to last figure (opposite page) is turned toward the church, continuing the inward movement of the portal.

MEDIEVAL ITALIAN PALACES

The gradual assertion of independent communes over imperial claims also had significant effects on the organization of medieval towns with their constantly growing populations and economies. The *duomo*, or cathedral, the symbolic and functional center of religious power, was now flanked by the *palazzo pubblico* or town hall, which responded to the new governmental and representational needs and which, as a town's second pole sanctioned the existing differentiation between the two seats of religious and secular power.
Previously, public meetings had been held in churches or in the open, in front of them. In northern Italy, the town hall was called the *broletto*, a word derived from *brolo* which means courtyard or enclosed field. The *broletto* has a large open portico on to the public square and leads via an external flight of steps up to a single room, usually frescoed.
The larger number of windows and the presence of balconies or steps are indicative of a gradual move away from types of construction derived from fortresses.

powerful Benedictines, Cluniacs and Cistercians, and built fortresses and palaces for noblemen and kings.

The monastic churches built in the Gothic period adopted similar principles to architectural principles cathedrals: a ground plan in the shape of a Latin cross, ratios and proportions tending toward the vertical, and construction methods using pointed rib vaults and arches and flying buttresses. Cistercian monasteries, however, are usually situated in isolated positions, far from towns, and, in keeping with austere monastic traditions, they were given very little decoration and no sculpture. The church, usually connected to a square cloister and the monastic buildings, is simple and bare

Above
Detail of the portico of the town hall in Piacenza.

Left
Palazzo del Bargello, Florence.
Square in shape with crenellations and a high tower, this was built for the Capitano del Popolo in 1255, extended in the 14th century and designated the residence of the Podestà, then of the Bargello. Today it houses Italy's richest museum of sculpture.

Below
Palazzo del Popolo, Orvieto.

Right
The broletto in Como. An interesting example of a light structure, further softened by the color effect produced by the alternating polychrome bands of marble.

Topographical defense
In medieval towns the houses, no longer built in wood but in stone or brick, were built directly overlooking the streets; fronts were narrow, developing upward and topped with a steeply sloping roof, especially in northern Europe where the climate was harsh.

Opposite page
Palazzo Vecchio in Florence, built between 1299 and 1314.

Left
A street in Mont-St-Michel, France. Medieval towns were surrounded by high walls and usually had an irregular plan; the streets followed the lie of the land and, because they were often set on a hill for defensive reasons, they were narrow, winding up and down.

although the accent on verticality remains. The technique employed for ecclesiastical buildings served as a model and stimulus to the development of secular architecture: castles, houses, bridges, town halls often flanked by a high tower and hospitals built for confraternities and charitable institutions. In towns fortified with great walls the urban plan was varied and irregular, the narrow winding streets following the natural slope of the terrain. Houses were increasingly made of stone rather than wood, especially those of noblemen, designed to be quickly transformed into miniature fortresses should the need arise (as it frequently did in those days), and built with the shortest side overlooking the street with a large main entrance. At the bottom an arcade enclosed the shops and stores; the rooms used by the nobleman's family were on the upper floors. The finest example of large Gothic civil architecture is the

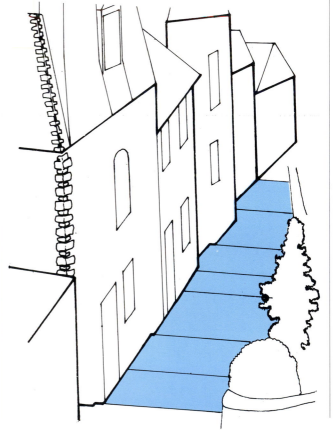

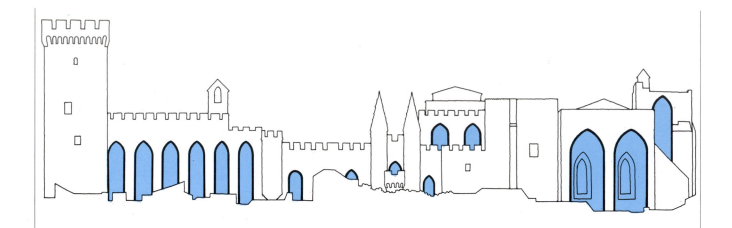

The fortified Holy See

Although the New Palace built for Pope Clement VI by Jean de Loubières (1342-1352) is also fortified, it has a more elegant appearance than the older parts of the building. The different construction concepts that inspired the two parts of the building are particularly visible in the contrasting window structures: those of the Old Palace are small, slit-like openings set high up and well protected whereas those of the New Palace are larger, and brighter, seemingly inspired by those of cathedrals and with no battlements. The construction methods used were the same as for the great cathedrals (with the addition of the walls needed for defense).

Palace of the Popes in Avignon, comprising the austere Old Palace (built by Pierre Poisson for Benedict XII) and the more elegant New Palace (built by Jean de Loubières for Clement VI).
The palace was intended to be as light and airy as a cathedral but these were hard times for the popes who often had to defend themselves with armed force, and the structure built by the architects is more like a fortress: the walls are massive and the windows are small narrow slits. Large pointed niches lend movement and upward height to the building, which has square towers at the corners, topped with projecting crenellated look-out towers; the most important, the Angel Tower, defended the papal

apartments.
Inside, the palace has a splendid courtyard leading to the apartments of the various members of the pope's household and the chapel.
The elegant and sumptuous rooms, decorated with frescoes and sculptures, are in sharp contrast to the military appearance of the building.
Gothic military

Below and detail left
The Palace of the Popes, Avignon.
The Old Palace, built between 1336 and 1342, surrounded by high walls with square towers at the corners. The Angel Tower (far right) contains the building's most sumptuous rooms, the pope's apartments.

architecture naturally responded more to practical than to artistic requirements. Defense was conceived as passive resistance behind strong walls so fortresses had high crenellated towers and bastions, walls with walkways for guards, and slit windows to protect the crossbowmen and other defenders, who poured burning oil or pitch down on attackers. Of particular interest is Castel del Monte in Puglia, a fine example of military architecture.

Above
Castello Estense, Ferrara.

Below
Castello San Giorgio, Mantua.

Left
Castello Visconteo, Pavia.

The fortress

A typical example of Gothic military architecture in which the towers protrude to avoid blind corners and to ensure that the attackers are always under fire.

The plan of the particularly severe Castel del Monte is based on a circle, although the structure is actually octagonal. The great ring of walls is octagonal, as are the large inner courtyard and the towers at the angles.

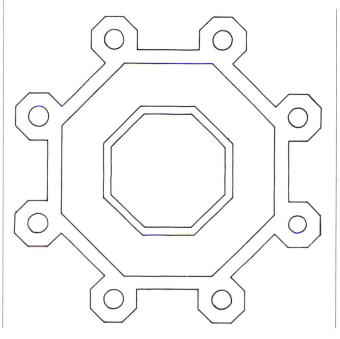

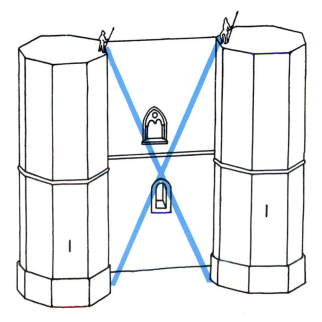

SCULPTURE

Undulation

Simeon and a servant, two statues on the central portal, dedicated to the Virgin, of the west front of Reims cathedral. The curvilinear fall of the draperies is obtained by shifting the axis of the servant's figure, with the weight borne on one leg.

Above

Arnolfo di Cambio, Virgin of the Nativity; *Florence, Museo dell'Opera del Duomo.*

Above

Maestro Antelamico, The Prophet Ezekiel, *detail; Parma, Baptistery.*

Below

Virgin and Child, *Fontenay Abbey.*

Monumental Gothic sculpture was mainly used on cathedral exteriors while interiors had almost none. It reproduced the characteristic vertical effect of the architecture in elongated figures, framed in niches closed with columns and crowned with canopies, rigid postures and garments falling in parallel lines like the

Above left
Tino di Camaino. Charity; Florence, Bardini Museum. This lyrical but realistic work combines the desire for solemnity of form with a more restless expressiveness, swaying between a classical sculptural quality and Gothic dynamism, characteristic of this sculptor who always obtained results of disarming beauty.

Above right and below
Giovanni di Balduccio, Tomb of Peter Martyr; Milan, church of Sant'Eustorgio. Assistants made this masterpiece by the sculptor between 1335 and 1339. The reliefs adorning the sarcophagus, eight scenes from the life of St. Peter Martyr, have crowded compositions with expressive figures and frequent repetition of poses.

A figure of a saint in the carved decoration of the Portal of the Martyrs at the cathedral of Notre-Dame, Chartres. This is a typical Gothic column statue in high relief on the column itself, accentuating the upward height.

Absolute verticality

This saint presents several characteristic features of Gothic art: an elongated figure; a canopy and pedestal framing it; arms held close to the body; rigid, parallel drapery folds that are as shallow as the fluting on a column; the head size respects the aesthetic criteria of the period (one-sixth of the length of the body); and a serene expression to convey the sanctity of the figure.

fluting on a column. Heads are more "alive," turned left or right leaning forward or tilted back. The facial features are formally represented for easy recognition by the onlooker: St. Firmin is a solemn and stately bishop, St. Elizabeth appears an elderly woman with a somewhat resigned air, and the Virgin Mary radiates youthful beauty. Most statues of the Virgin Mary, and female figures in general, are elongated and often curvilinear, sometimes even to the degree of forming an S shape. As well as large cathedral statues, the theme of the Virgin and

Giovanni Pisano, Sibyl, *Siena, Museo dell'Opera del Duomo.*

Bonino da Campione, Burial Monument of Barnabò Visconti; *Milan, Castello Sforzesco, Civic Museums.*

THE RELIEFS OF ORVIETO CATHEDRAL

The reliefs covering the bottom of the second and third piers of the façade of Orvieto cathedral reveal in iconography and motifs the influence of Nicola and Giovanni Pisano. One depicts a series of *Messianic Prophecies* and the other *Episodes from the Life of Jesus.* The reliefs date from just before 1310 and precede those portraying *Scenes from Genesis* and a large *Last Judgment.* They are probably the work of the Sienese artist Lorenzo Maitani (though some say of an Umbrian-Sienese given the explanatory name of *"Maestro Sottile,"* who was master builder of the cathedral without interruption from 1310 to 1330 and, in 1321, was paid for the bronze cast of an eagle, the symbol of John the Evangelist, on the cathedral's façades. On all four piers scenes of small figures are framed by elegant vines and foliage, giving them the appearance of huge illuminated pages. The subjects chosen make them among the most original and organic narrative and symbolic ensembles of the 14th century. Although the different languages adopted by the most important masters who succeeded one another here and the lack of records pose as yet unresolved problems of historical and stylistic qualification, no one can deny the Sienese character, at least of the reliefs on the first and fourth piers, as the fine, delicate rhythm of composition and linear fluency of the figures correspond, in some aspects, to the contemporary painting of that school (in the picture *Stories from the New Testament,* third pier on the façade).

Child was a favorite for small statues produced by craftsmen for country churches and for the private use of the aristocracy and wealthy merchants. Most frequently these images portrayed the Virgin and Child, although subject matter also included Christ and St. John (the disciple asleep on the breast of the Redeemer), the *Pietà* (the dead Christ lying in Mary's arms) and the Crucifixion.

These sculptural types led to the series of *Die Schönen Madonnen*, a number of elegantly modeled sculptures depicting the Virgin and Child by Bohemian and German craftsmen, of which perhaps the finest example is the masterpiece known as the Virgin of Krumau. For a better understanding of Gothic sculpture it must be remembered that it was always painted. Faces and hands were given a natural color and the hair was golden blond; robes were brightly colored and jewels, clasps and the edges of mantels were encrusted with precious stones or colored glass. The effect was that of a truly celestial vision.

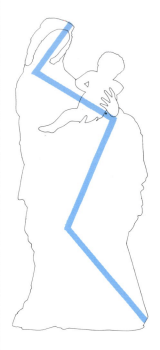

The Virgin of Krumau; Vienna, Kunsthistorisches Museum.
This small sculpture (112 cm) was made in or around 1400 at Krumau in Bohemia and extensively copied in central Europe. As all Gothic sculptures, it was painted and preserves traces of the original colors.

Zigzag
The tension between the broken lines, typical of free standing sculptures articulates this Virgin and Child – perhaps the most popular subject for small statues, devotional images destined for private worship; the whole composition is softened by the elegant draperies.

Opposite page
Giovanni Pisano, the pulpit in Pisa cathedral.

APPLIED ARTS

Historians and art critics, in order to distinguish stained glass, jewelery, illuminated manuscripts, and tapestry from the main arts of architecture, sculpture, and painting, use the term "applied arts." During the Gothic period some of these minor arts, such as that of stained-glass windows, reached heights that would never again be equalled. There were social and economic reasons for the profusion of these arts. During the later Middle Ages the life style of rich merchants started to rival that of the nobility. They commissioned jewelery, tapestries, small paintings, and illuminated manuscripts for their homes and left the artists greater freedom in the choice of subject and execution than had been granted by the clergy and nobility, previously their usual and only clients.

The extraordinary development of stained-glass windows was due to their extensive use in cathedrals to create amazing and almost impalpable walls. The window was made by cutting small pieces from panes of colored glass and joining them with strips of lead to a design prepared by an artist. Facial features were delicately painted in as were other details in each figure, such as the folds of garments. The individual scenes making up a large composition were enclosed within a frame, usually multifoiled. Each frame contained a scene from the Old or New Testament and was intended to educate the

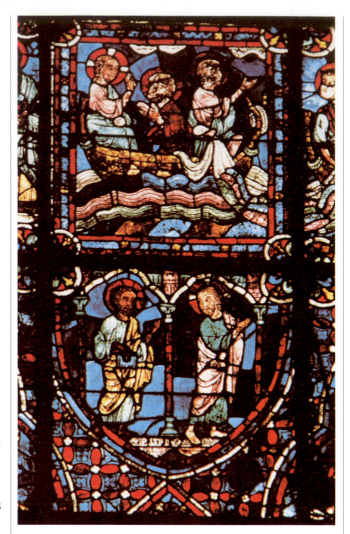

Opposite page
*Detail of a large
stained-glass window in
Notre-Dame, Chartres,
depicting episodes from the
life of Christ. The scenes
are arranged in sequence.*

Stained glass
*Typically Gothic
stained-glass windows
present an extreme wealth
of detail, clear-cut figures in
poses that facilitate
identification and an
architectural background or
one of stylized motifs from
nature.*

Right
Ugolino Vieri, The Corporal
Reliquary, *1337/38; Orvieto
cathedral.*

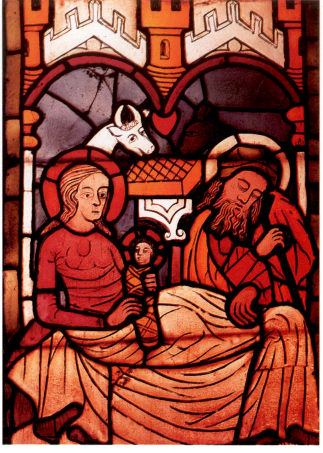

worshiper. Clarity was achieved by keeping the number of figures to a bare minimum, elongated and two-dimensional, that is with height and width but no depth. Expression was conveyed less by the face and more by gestures, accentuated to make each scene quite clear.
Backgrounds were also two-dimensional, with an occasional indication of depth (a characteristic found in all Gothic painting). The setting was suggested by architectural features (pointed arches resting on small columns), a hint of landscape (stylized rocks and trees) or the sea (again extremely stylized in a series of wavy lines one above the other). The design was extremely sophisticated and even the tiniest details were executed with great precision. The makers of

Above left
Adoration of the Magi, *stained-glass window from the island of Gotland (Sweden); Stockholm, National Museum.*

Above right
Nativity, *a stained-glass window from the island of Gotland (Sweden); Stockholm, National Museum.*

Below left
Detail of the *Life of the Virgin, stained-glass window in Chartres cathedral.*

Below right
Crucifixion, *stained-glass window in Sens cathedral.*

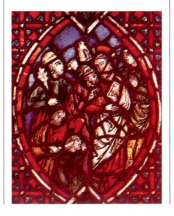

stained-glass windows – masters at producing works that would be viewed from a considerable distance – rivalled the illuminators of manuscripts for fine precision and grace. Colors were usually bold: reds, blues, greens, and yellows all combined with an extraordinary sense of color harmony. Equally precious (partly for the materials employed) was the jewelery made by

Gothic goldsmiths. The expansion of this art is not explained solely by the love of luxury of kings, noblemen, wealthy classes and clergy; it also had a philosophical motivation. For medieval man precious material symbolized the spiritual value of an object, and most of the production of the period was destined for religious use. It included ceremonial vessels (chalices and pyxes),

Detail of the Pala d'Oro; Venice, San Marco. This large and complex work (3.50 x 2.10 m) in gold and gilded silver studded with jewels, most now lost, encloses 83 enamels with figures as well as numerous other small medallions. A work of Byzantine style, technique and production, the enamels belong to different periods but most are older than the complete remake of the altarpiece ordered in the first half of the 14th century.

THE GOLDSMITH'S ART IN SIENA

The city of Siena played a particular role in the 14th century thanks to the great specialization developed by its goldsmiths, a technique often associated with the ancient working of enamel. They perfected a procedure by which sheet silver was worked in bas-relief with low-cut figures. The rest of Europe adopted the *champlevé* technique in which cells are cut away in the plate; enamel is then added and left opaque to hide abnormalities. The new procedures employed in Siena allowed the use of translucent enamel, which would thus also enrich the chasing of the base with color. The artistic works produced by Sienese goldsmiths, one of the oldest being a chalice made by Guccio di Manaia between 1288 and 1292 and preserved in the church of San Francesco in Assisi, show the influence of northern Gothic art, stimulated by the techniques of stained-glass windows, goldsmithery and illumination in general.

127

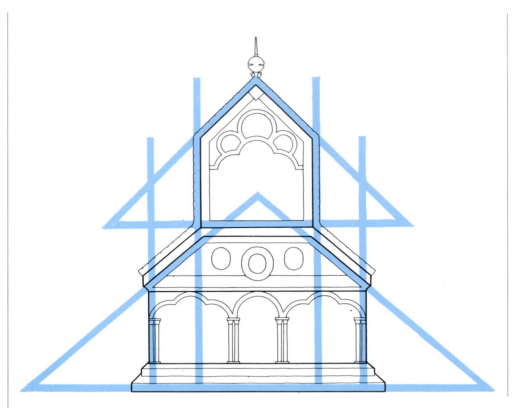

Geometry
Gothic artists found particular inspiration in geometric shapes (circles, equilateral triangles, rectangles and polygons). The structure of this reliquary (which reproduces that of a basilica) is easily broken down into a series of such shapes.

The reliquary of the Three Kings made by the goldsmith Nicolas of Verdun between 1180 and 1230; Cologne cathedral. In keeping with a commonly adopted formula, the plan of the reliquary copies that of a basilica with three aisles. It is 170 cm wide and 180 cm long.

reliquaries, and monstrances.

Gold and silver objects of this kind were the pride of many a cathedral or sanctuary treasury. Most have now been dispersed having represented too great a temptation to the powerful over the centuries, who vied with each other to possess them. The pieces were often encrusted with pearls, precious stones and rock crystals and decorated with filigree work and enamel. Architecture – spires, flying buttresses and an exaggerated sense of verticality – usually inspired the creators of Gothic gold-work, and reliquaries and monstrances often look like precious models of buildings. One of the best-known works of the period is the reliquary of the Three Kings, by Nicholas of Verdun. This oak casket is made in the shape of a basilica with a high nave flanked by two lower aisles. The outer covering is of embossed and gilded silver and faithfully reproduces a church exterior. The shorter sides are decorated just like church façades and the longer ones have a number of arches on small piers (like the arches of a nave) containing the figures of apostles, prophets, or kings.

The images are elongated in keeping

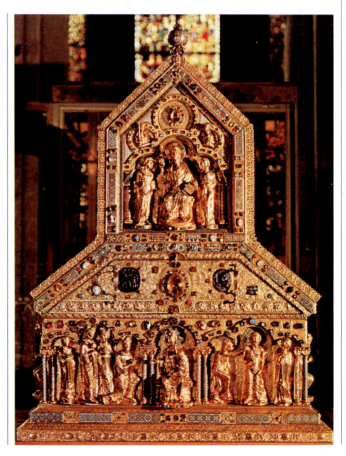

Reliquary of the head of St. Galgano, 1290-1300, in copper and silver gilt embossed and chased; Siena, Museo dell'Opera del Duomo.

Two dimensions

The Gothic style featured the surface definition of the scene against a two-dimensional background decorated with abstract motifs, resembling fabric, and between stylized supports. The most important person was in the center. The absence of a sense of perspective was so marked that the feet of the figures (to the fore) sometimes overlapped.

Manuscript illumination depicting Charlemagne sending Gano to the queens of Saragossa, taken from the Chroniques de Saint-Denis. *These illustrations with profane subjects have essentially narrative purposes and enrich the text like proper illustrations. The exaggerated mimicry of the gestures and facial expressions produces maximum clarity of expression.*

with the canons of monumental sculpture and perfectly inserted into the architectural features (the arches) used to circumscribe the scenes.

The art of illumination also reached a degree of originality and excellence never equaled afterward. Illuminations were painted on the parchment of manuscripts – printing had not yet been invented or was, at any rate, still unknown outside China.

The best known and most important center of this art form was Paris, although the greatest artists of this school were actually Flemish. Its development was bound with the increased distribution of illuminated manuscripts, previously almost exclusively found in monasteries. As occurred for other forms of Gothic art, growing prosperity and cultural changes created a demand among private patrons, aristocrats and the wealthy.

Illuminators were now called upon to decorate books that, though still large, were smaller and

Illuminated page of the Maciejowice Psalter, circa 1250, Ms. 638, f. 39; New York, Pierpont Morgan Library.

Above left
Yves de Saint-Denis, Messengers Sent to Rome, *illumination from the* Life of St. Denis; *Paris, Bibliothèque Nationale.*

Left
Jean Pucelle, Saul Trying to Wound David, *illumination from the* Belleville Breviary; *Paris, Bibliothèque Nationale.*

Love of nature
The month of June, an illumination taken from Tres Riches Heures du Duc de Berry, *a famous manuscript decorated by the brothers Pol, Hannequin and Hermant de Limbourg and completed* by Jean Colombe in 1485; *Chantilly, Musée Condé. There is greater attention here to the landscape, viewed in fleeting perspective: the background is defined in detail and no longer only alluded to with stylized motifs. This is based on the city of Paris, the Palais de la Cité and Ste-Chapelle, as they appeared in the Middle Ages, being distinguishable in the background. The latter is not sacrificed to the image of the harvest to the fore and is executed with such love of detail that, if isolated, it becomes a picture in its own right.*

more manageable
(practically the "pocket"
editions of the times).
These were books of
psalms, books of hours
(prayer books) or
missals for private use,
which indicated the
services to be conducted
at various hours of the
day and night, and
manuscripts of secular
interest, such as
romantic epics, tales,
chronicles and
collections of songs.
Gothic illuminations
served both decorative
and narrative functions.
The ornamentation of
the capital letters

opening books or
chapters was purely
decorative and often
developed into linear
arabesques that framed
the entire page. Motifs
were usually taken from
the plant and animal
kingdoms and included
stylized designs of
flowers, birds, or
insects. Full-page
illuminations directly
illustrated the text by
telling a story.
Sometimes the space
was divided into small
sections each containing
a scene, producing a
sequence of episodes on
one page. The individual

scenes might be
enclosed in quatrefoiled
frames giving the page
the appearance of a
stained-glass window,
an effect reinforced by
the use of bright colors.
The style of the
illuminations, as for
stained glass and
painting, was
two-dimensional, the
elegant and richly clad
figures often being
drawn against a gold
background with
minute precision. There
was a striking wealth
and variety in the
illustrations with
splendid colors and an

abundance of gold; as
previously mentioned,
to the medieval mind, a
precious exterior was a
sign of the spiritual and
religious value of the
book's contents. The
subject of the
illuminations, however,
was not always
religious. The
masterpiece *Très Riches
Heures*, the Book of
Hours of the Duke of
Berry, contains a series
of scenes depicting
agricultural toil, towns,
crafts and other scenes
taken from everyday life
in minute and exquisite
detail.

Tapestries were also widely used during this period. These large woven textiles were of major importance in Gothic times and appealed to the refined tastes of the nobility. They were used to decorate the bare walls of big, cold rooms or to divide particularly large rooms to create a cosier atmosphere. Lay subjects were favored and included gallant and amorous adventures, hunting scenes, allegories and fabulous legends such as that of the Lady and the Unicorn. Some tapestries depicted religious subjects, and these were mostly used to adorn altars. In accordance with a characteristic trend of the times, stronger in the later period, holy stories were also placed in secular, worldly court settings. As a result biblical scenes and stories inspired by the lives of the saints were turned into images of striking elegance and refinement. The characters – Christ, the Virgin Mary, and martyrs – were given aristocratic features, their clothes and headgear resembling those used by the nobility; the architectural framework reproduced sumptuous interiors though always using fine lines, in keeping with the ethereal lightness of the figures.

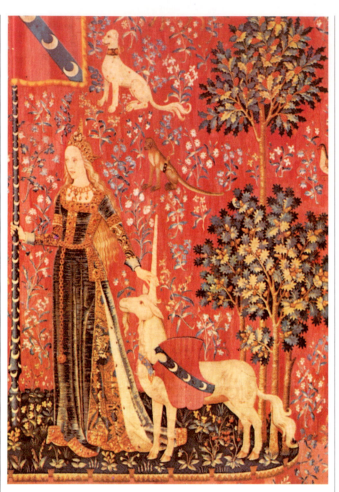

Heraldic taste

The height of the slender and aristocratic female figure (which reflects the principles of Gothic art) is accentuated by a number of vertical elements – the pole bearing the banner, the twisted horn on the animal's head and the woman's stiff posture – which contrast with the softer lines of the unicorn. Curiously, the shield and banner both bear the arms of the family that commissioned the tapestry, the La Vistas.

One of the Lady and the Unicorn *tapestries, Paris, Musée Cluny. The cycle of six pieces, late works, originally decorated a room in Boussac castle. The use of color is highly unusual, with the ruby red background creating a striking and daring contrast with the deep blue area, a sort of small island, on* which the figures are placed. There is no perspective and the composition is like a patchwork of areas of clearly defined color.

PAINTING

During the Gothic period painting did not, on the whole, play as fundamental a role as in many other periods of art history. Because there was so little solid, unbroken wall space in Gothic cathedrals, they did not lend themselves to painted decoration. The great cycles of narrative frescoes disappeared from church walls although Italy was an exception; here Gothic architecture never attained the soaring verticality and lightness of the French, English, and German churches and the taste for major frescoed works based on religious subjects survived. Painting was, however, widely used for secular purposes, to decorate the rooms of castles, aristocratic homes and civic buildings. There was an economic reason for this, in that fresco was a cheaper decorative wall covering than tapestry. Heroic tales and scenes from life at court were popular subjects.

At this time in Europe the most popular religious paintings were on panels; noblemen and the wealthy commissioned small panels or portable altars for their religious worship and the clergy

Above
Ambrogio Lorenzetti, Allegory of Good Government, *detail; Siena, Palazzo Pubblico.*

Bottom left
Giotto, Driving the Devils out of Arezzo *(after restoration); Assisi, upper church of San Francesco.*

Opposite page
Simple elegance
Stefan Lochner, Adoration of the Child; *Munich, Alte Pinakothek. This small* picture (36 x 23 cm) is an example of paintings intended for private worship. The composition – typically Gothic in technique (tempera on wood), the attention to detail and the elegant posture of the Virgin – is greatly simplified, as the customary figures of St. Joseph and the Three Kings are absent.

had larger works
executed for the
churches. These were
either displayed on the
altarpiece as a single
panel or consisted of
several hinged panels,
called a polyptych. The
latter came to be the
most popular form of
Gothic painting and was
its most typical
expression. They are
large works made up of
several panels brought
together; those with two
panels are known as
diptychs and those with
three triptychs. Each
panel was framed by a
pointed arch, sometimes
having three lobes,
resting on slender
columns – very similar
in appearance to a
Gothic window. The
frequent use of
pinnacles, spires and
flower motifs to
decorate the frame
further recalls the
architecture of the time.
As in the case of
illumination, Gothic
painting paid great
attention to detail but

demonstrated little interest in perspective. A background of gold often surrounded the foreground figures, creating a celestial atmosphere and, at the same time, enhancing the other colors. Gothic painters were more concerned with rendering the spiritual and divine aspects than with realism produced by the spatial depth of a third dimension. The faces, especially those of the women, are gentle, serene and slightly stylized as if the artist were copying an ideal prototype. These figures inhabit a world of grace, beauty, balance, and calm where sin, pain and the vulgarity of daily life no longer exist. Of course the outside world

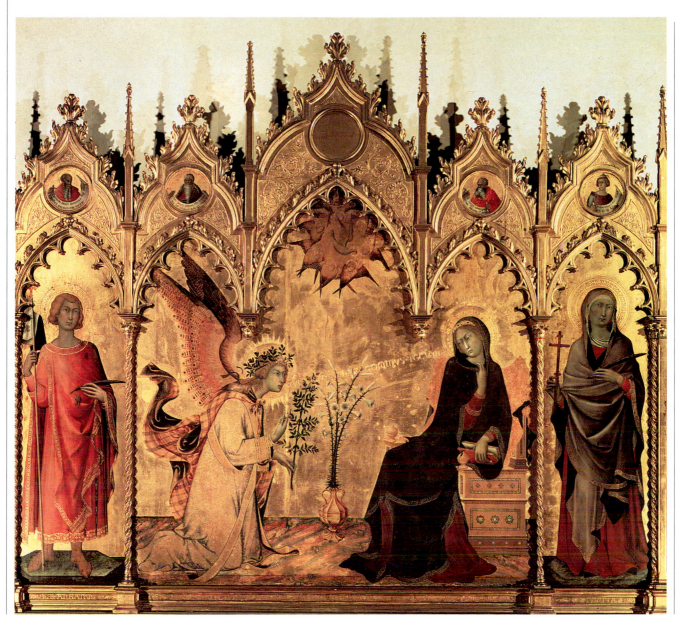

POLYPTYCHS

Between the late 13th and early 14th centuries Italian artists invented the polyptych, an architectural composition of painted panels grouped in a carved and gilded wooden frame. The polyptych has no standard type. The shape, size and number of panels vary according to its intended function, the client's or maker's taste and the geographical area of its production. The most common 14th-century type has a number of aligned panels, vertical in format and curved to a point, odd in number (usually three, five or seven), the central one being larger than those at the sides. Beneath each panel is a painted rectangular panel, set horizontally: the predella. This basic arrangement was, however, subjected to numerous variations in the two centuries during which polyptychs were produced, between the early 14th and the early 16th centuries. The panels were sometimes joined with hinges to form small altars, usually diptychs or triptychs, which could be folded and easily moved. These were extremely useful for private worship. There has been a disastrous systematic dismantling and dismembering of polyptychs; this started in the 1600s but has been especially common since the 19th century with altarpieces being removed from churches and destined for private collections by dealers who increase their profits by dividing them up for individual sale. Panels that were made to stand together have been dispersed to the collections and museums of different cities, nations and continents. Although this may not lessen the individual quality of the painting, the importance of a polyptych lies in the harmony of form and color created by the panels together and in relation to the frame. Division leads to the loss of essential documentary, aesthetic and historical details (in the photograph: Giovanni da Milano, *Polyptych*; Prato, Pinacoteca comunale).

is not like this, but the artist cancels the reality around him, that which he sees every day. He presents ideal, aristocratic figures, Virgins in flowing robes that fall in ample and elegant folds, curved lines that convey a love of geometry (the favorite subjects of Stefan Lochner and Simone Martini), chaste valiant knights wearing shining armor and splendidly dressed prelates kneeling in prayer. As a rule these figures were given a stylized architectural background, but even when the artist introduced natural elements in the form of rocks, trees, or flowers to create an atmosphere these were reproduced in a fairly schematic manner.

There were of course exceptions to the most typical features of Gothic painting described, the most important being Giotto (1267-1337) whose work focused on the expression of the human drama and destiny. His Crucifix in the church of Santa Maria Novella, in Florence, did indeed

Opposite page
Human substance
Giotto di Bondone, Crucifixion; *Florence, Santa Maria Novella. Christ's body is set in a curve that comprises the reclining head and is countered by the extended arms. Distancing himself, as the head of a school should, from the usual artistic canons of Gothic,* Giotto is unconcerned with linear rhythms and purely aesthetic values but represents solid figures, arranged in depth, stressing Christ's suffering with great attention to anatomy, achieved with the use of chiaroscuro. The colors are less bright than those normally used by Gothic artists.

portray the figure of Christ on the cross with the half figures of Mary and John flanking him. However, the figure of the dying Christ is made more human. Instead of concentrating on decorative value, Giotto strives to lend corporeal substance.

The colors are subdued and full of shadow; the face, bowed on the chest, expresses suffering. The normally bright and refined colors of a Gothic painting sometimes become intense. This is the case of the *Resurrection of Christ,* painted by an anonymous Bohemian painter known as the Master of Trebon or Wittingau (circa 1380). The composition is based on a daring combination of red and green that produces a fantastic, almost visionary effect and is enhanced by a red sky dotted with gold stars. Similar examples show the unreal, dreamlike atmosphere that is a constant presence in European Gothic painting, in one form or another: fairytale wonder, mystical spirituality or gallant legend.

Unreality
The background of sloping rocks with small stylized trees is a characteristic of the Gothic style, as is the vertical rendering of the slender figure of the risen Christ, accentuated by the presence of the staff with the cross. Equally typical is the erect figure of Christ dominating the painting, while his enemies, symbolizing the forces of evil, appear defeated and are relegated to secondary positions away from the center of the composition.

Master of Trebon or Wittingau, Resurrection of Christ; *Prague, National Gallery. Executed around 1380, this was a panel of the altar of Wittingau, after which the anonymous painter is named.*
The composition is based on a bold combination of red and green, the effect being heightened by a red sky dotted with gold stars.

Opposite page
Simone Martini, St. Martin's Investiture as a Knight *from the* Life of St. Martin; *Assisi, lower church of San Francesco.*